a cottage in donegal

Mary Doherty's Story

Eva Doherty Gremmert

First Published 2011 by HBG Services, Inc, Carnation
First Printing 2011 by Western Type & Printing,

ISBN 978-0-578-08012-3

Much appreciation and many thanks to Warren Funnell
of Western Type & Printing, Lynnwood WA, for his
valuable suggestions and his excellent professional
technical services.

To my dad.
You took me to Ireland for the first time.
I miss you.

contents

**Portraits of Paddy and Mary Doherty
taken in 1903, they hang on Eva's front room wall.**

acknowledgements

It would be impossible for me to mention everyone who has helped me with the research for this book. I am eternally grateful to each and every person who has guided me.

First I must mention my wonderful husband Arden, who carefully helped me prepare the final manuscript with his exacting proofreading. If you find anything, you must tell him. I mention with gratitude the time and patience shown me by three cousins: Josie "Paul", Susan from Pendleton, and Liam "Derry Bill". Throughout their lives, they kept our history. While they were still with us, they were patient with me as I wrote down everything they were telling me. I miss my visits with them and think of them fondly still.

Cousin Roger from Blackhorse was the first to mention that 'someone' should write the family history back in 1976 and challenged me to do it. Thank you Roger, it has been a great journey. His sister Martha still continues to collect pictures, stories and artifacts so that we can be connected to our Irish history and family heritage.

Cousins in Ireland, Oregon, New York and California have assisted me in gathering the stories. Here's to all the Dohertys, including, John and Moira "Saddler", Joe "Paul" and Mary, Mary Christina and Luke, Rosemary "Paul", John and Gemma, and many others. The Book Shop, Carndonagh has the best collection of Irish books, including many hard to find ones. I appreciate their help and the gentle suggestions of other books I might want to look at. I have gathered a fine collection. My reading inspired my writing.

Irish historians and academics have been very encouraging, especially Sean Beattie, historian and editor of the Donegal Historical Society Annual. Irish storyteller and author, Hazel McIntyre, taught me valuable lessons about the creative process and the discipline of writing.

Over the past year, I invited several close friends to read the manuscript before publishing. The insight I received from each reader has been invaluable. I am grateful for their time, thoughtful comments and suggestions.

The photographs are from our many family trips to the auld sod. My sister Rosie is a very talented artist. Her drawings of the cottage, the ship and the woman spinning are incredible. I know that you will enjoy them.

Most of all, I want to thank Mary herself for the legacy that she has passed on to all of us. Her story needed to be told.

FOREWORD

This book, "A Cottage in Donegal," is a work of historical fiction. It is the story of Mary Doherty, my great-grandmother, who lived her entire life in the same townland in County Donegal, Ireland. In my own childhood home, the large portraits of Mary and her husband Paddy, taken in 1903 hung on the wall of the front room. Mary has always intrigued me. After I married, my father gave me the portraits. Now they hang on the wall by my own front door.

This book, written in memoir form, is from Mary's perspective. There are no surviving letters or journals from Mary herself. I have created an entertaining, historically accurate story of the life of a typical woman in rural Ireland in the 19th century from family stories and the remaining artifacts from Mary's life. Over the past 25 years, I have made multiple trips each year to Ireland for research. Many people are intrigued with Post-Famine Ireland. As I reviewed my own extensive library, as well as the collections of others, I discovered that there were not many books written from a woman's perspective. I decided to write a book about the time period in which Mary Doherty lived. During her lifetime, Ireland changed dramatically and my story reflects those changes.

My great-grandparents posterity now numbers over 600 people. Their legacy circles the globe, from Ireland, England, Wales, Scotland, Canada, and the US, including New York, Washington DC, Nevada, Colorado, Alaska, California, Oregon, and Washington. Over the years, as I have met each of my cousins descended from Mary and Paddy, I have come to recognize the common values of family, hard work, and integrity that have been passed down through the generations regardless of the different cultures in which we have lived. I have self-published five family history books. This is my first work of fiction.

Eva Doherty Gremmert – March 2011

glossary

Banshee – a tradition that this sound heralds the imminent death of someone from the house. This witch sometimes appears as a young woman or an old hag.

Big House – a term referring to the large homes owned by the landed gentry, the landlords or nobility.

Brachán House. Brachán is cooked corn gruel. The words "corn meal" refer to any cereal grain. From 1846 to 1849 there was a very large pot of meal cooked everyday at the Brachán House to feed anyone who had a need.

Brae – road that either goes up or down a hill or incline.

Brehon laws - the ancient laws that governed Ireland prior to the English occupation of Ireland. Women were the equal of men, and could vote, own property and even govern when called upon.

Brógaí – commonly hobnail boots, also the Irish word for shoes.

Byre – a shelter for cows. The barn was an outlying farm building used for storing grain or animal heed and housing farm animals.

Ceili – traditional Irish folk dance and entertainment, where musicians would play and the locals would gather to entertain themselves.

Chuffed – proud or pleased about something, such as a parents feelings toward a childs' good accomplishments.

Cleavers – is an edible and medicinal herb. See the description in the Medicinal Remedies list.

Consumption – a disease commonly known as tuberculosis.

Corn - In Ireland, corn is a general term for all grains and cereal crops, typically oats. Maize or Indian Corn was imported from America, and was difficult to grind in local mills. It did not gain popularity as cattle feedstuff until after the Famine time.

Corpse-house – the house is called a corpse-house while a wake is being held. It is commonly pronounced corp-house.

Craic – the fun or good times, like at a party or a gathering.

Crane – the L-shaped iron holder for the cookpot to be suspended over the open fire. Sometimes it had a hook on the end to hold the pot.

Cratur – locally illegal home-brewed distilled poitin (liquor) is often called 'a drop of the cratur.'

Currach – the small boat made out of animal skins or hide, used by local fishermen both as a sea boat and a vessel for inland waters.

Decade of the Rosary – in the Catholic religion, "saying the Rosary" is the practice of saying an "Our Father" prayer, then 10 "Hail Mary" prayers followed by a "Glory Be to the Father" prayer. This is repeated five times to make a decade or set whilst counting on a string of prayer beads called the Rosary.

The Diamond – the center of the village, similar to the town square or green in England.

Dulse Seaweed– an edible form of algae growing widely along the shoreline of the North Atlantic. It is dried and typically purple in colour.

Earnest or Earl – a pledge at the hiring fairs between the child's parents and the farmer hiring them. It represented a contract for work.

Eegit – The Irish pronunciation of Idiot, sounds like 'ee-jit'.

The Famine or Big Hunger – the period in Irish history from 1846 – 1849 when the potato crop failed because of the blight and millions of Irish died or emigrated to avoid starvation.

Fine Folks – those individuals of high birth or born into wealth, land owners that lived in the Big Houses – The gentry.

Flactering – In harvesting turf, flactering is peeling back the sod to expose the underlying turf.

Handy-woman – a local woman who helped in times of birth and death. She worked as a mid-wife and as a mortician.

Jumper – a common name for a pullover sweater, typically handmade.

Keeners – women who weep, wail and sing over a body at the corpse-house and in the funeral.

Kenters – stall salesmen, especially during a fair day, would call out to passerby's attempting to attract attention to their wares.

Loghters – the name given to the armfuls of grain each man could collect while harvesting.

Meals

       Breakfast – the morning meal, usually porridge.

       Dinner – the main meal of the day, served in the middle of the day.

       Tea – the evening meal, usually a light meal served with a cup of tea.

Meitheal - The party at the end of the harvest. The word is an Irish word that means a gang of workmen working together to harvest any crop and may not include a feast.

Men of Fashion – the fine folk, the men that lived in the Big Houses.

Messages – is used to mean running errands, or having a list to do while in town including shopping, as in 'going to get the messages'.

Midgies – are tiny biting flies that are active from mid-May to September particularly when it is calm and overcast. The bites can lead to swelling and intense itching.

Mind – in Ireland this means the same as remember, such as 'I mind the time…'.

Mingin' – minging means dirty as in clothing.

The Necessary – the outdoor toilet or privy.

Penal Times – The Penal Laws were passed in the 17th and 18th centuries. They outlawed the practice of the Catholic religion, enacted strict penalties, including loss of property ownership, loss of inheritance, and in some instances, even death. Catholics could not hold public office or serve in the army. They had to pay 'recusant fines' for non-attendance at

Protestant church services. Roman Catholic churches were transferred to the Protestant Church of Ireland. Everyone regardless of religious affiliation was subject to the paying of tithes to the established church, later called the Church of Ireland. After the Tithe War period of 1831 – 1836, the tithes were reduced, later they were added to the land rents and finally they were completely abolished in 1869.

Pin Money – money a woman earned through her labour, selling such things as eggs, butter or hand-work. The money was for her separate use.

Poitín – the illegal liquor brewed in handmade stills in the hills.

Praties – Potatoes.

Prospect – the view out over the landscape.

Reading the Banns – custom of announcing a couple's intent to wed to the local community. These were read out during the church service over a few weeks, so that anyone needing to could raise their objections to the marriage.

Rear up on – to shout at, usually regarding disciplining children.

Remains – the corpse is often called the remains during the wake, funeral up to the burial.

Retting the Flax – soaking the reeds in water. This begins to rot the woody fibres and softens them enough to be able to further process the flax.

Ritting – to cut a line down through the sod to begin the process of harvesting turf.

Row – to have a fight, usually including verbal exchanges.

Sally Garden – the kitchen garden, next to the house, tended and managed by the woman of the house. A sally is a willow tree, and they used withes of the willow tree to fasten thatching on roofs back in the old days in Ireland. Each village had a bush of willow trees on the outskirts, primarily to provide the necessary material for thatching, and this bush was called the sally gardens. It was also the 19th century equivalent of a lovers' lane, where the young folk would go to be alone. White Willow (Salix alba) Irish Sailach (Willows in general) (family - Salicaceae), Sailach - pronounced 'Sally'.

Shanachies - the clan historians who would tell the clan histories through song or tales.

Slipe – a horse drawn flat bed on runners, used to haul turf or crops from the fields.

Sloughs – the underground storage tanks for the slurry.

Stooks – during harvest seven to twelve sheaves are stacked together to make the stooks.

Tay – Another name for a cup of tea.

Traps – small horse carts, like a buggy.

Travelling People - the tinkers, they are nomadic people in Ireland. Tinkering or tinsmithing, the mending of tin ware such as pots and pans, were services traditionally associated with Irish Travellers.

Trousseau – a bride's possessions of clothing and household goods that she brought to the marriage.

Turf – the dried peat moss from the bog that is used for fuel, both heating and cooking.

Wake – a three day vigil, watching over a corpse, usually held in the home of the deceased.

Weans – children.

Wee Cupa – to share a cup of tea between friends, a social custom.

Whin bushes – The yellow flowering bushes sometimes used for hedging. The small bright yellow flower is dried and used as a dye for cloth and Easter eggs. It is also crushed, dried and fed to horses. It gives them great energy especially for heavy work such as plowing.

Whinge – crying, such as a child, commonly in the phrase, whingin' and whinin'.

Wooden Couples & Wooden Pins – roof rafters. The couples are held by the pins.

Chapter 1

Paddy Is Gone
Wednesday, 12 November 1919

Tonight my grief overwhelms me. I feel the need to write everything down so that I will not forget. For the first time in more than fifty years of marriage, the other side of my bed is cold and empty. As I reach out my hand, Paddy is not there.

He is gone since Monday morning and now he is buried in the churchyard down by the chapel.

I want to call out, "Where are you, where have you gone?"

But there would be no answer.

The only noises in the house are the muffled whispers of my son Paul and his wife Mary from their room above mine and their children rustling the bedclothes in their room across the hall upstairs. Even the chickens and sheep have gone to sleep. All is silent.

Last Sunday Paddy seemed so very tired. Typically he was a quiet man but that evening he was unusually quiet. After our evening tea I helped him change into his bedclothes and then tucked him into the bed. As I finished the usual preparations for night, he turned his face toward the sound of my moving about the room.

Sighing almost in a whisper, he called out my name, "Mary, come on over here to me."

I stepped closer and took his hands in mine. Although blind, his eyes seemed to seek my face.

"I am so very, very tired Mary, bone weary and cold."

I tried to make light of it.

"The weather has been that bad this last while, a good rest is what you need."

He got very quiet and I barely heard him say, "I think that very soon, I will have a long, long rest. This evening after our tea while you and Paul's Mary were cleaning up, I heard the banshee."

I told him not to speak thus, that it had been the wind whipping around the corner of the house. He again sighed, settled down into the bed and I thought he had fallen asleep.

As I brushed the floor, prepared the fire coals for night and turned down the lamp I thought about the traditions and legends surrounding the banshee. She is a fairy woman, an omen of death. She is thought to be an ancestral messenger appointed to forewarn members of the five major ancient Irish families. Since all O'Dochartaighs are descendants of Niall of the Nine hostages, we are eligible to receive this warning.

The banshee's appearance is not always the same. Usually she appears as an ugly, frightening hag, but she has been known to appear as a stunningly beautiful woman of any age. The hag can also appear as a washer-woman, seen washing the blood stained clothes of those who are about to die. She will wail around a house if someone in the house is about to die. This is what Paddy said that he heard. I dismissed my growing fear as nonsense and made ready for bed.

As I carefully climbed into our bed, he startled me when he spoke. "I want you to know that I have had a good life, Mary. You have been a good wife to me for all these many years."

Never before had I heard such talk from my husband. Then I snuggled down into the place that had been mine since the night of our marriage.

I patted his cheek and said, "Aye Paddy, we have had a good life together. Good night to ye."

Those were the last words we spoke to one another. When I awoke in the morning, he was already cold. I had missed his passing. I sat on the edge of the bed, with my back to him, silent tears streaming down my face and falling onto the bedclothes. I had yet to call out to Paul and Mary, to give them the sad news.

I took these few moments for my own, alone in my grief, the loneliness overwhelming me. I knew that as soon as it was known the busy-ness that surrounds death would start.

Paddy and I had lived through so much together. I had birthed our twelve children and we had buried two of them as weans. We watched over and loved the remaining ten and mourned them in turn as they each left our home and hearth to travel to America. We rejoiced with the two who returned to rear their families near and felt heartache for the rest of our grandchildren who would never know our voices.

I waited until the tears stopped, and taking a deep breath, I stood. Turning to look back, I noticed that he looked at peace. Tenderly I kissed his brow, smoothed the bedclothes around him and went to find my son Paul.

Within a few hours, Mary Ann McGuinness, the handy-woman from over the road came to help Mary and me wash his body and shave his face. Paul moved the kitchen table into the upper room and placed chairs around the house. With Paddy dressed in his best clothes, he was laid out on the table. The mirrors had been covered and the clock stopped indicating the time of death. The door to the cottage was opened which signaled to the neighbours that all had been made ready.

The wake was on for Monday and Tuesday with the funeral on Wednesday. During that time the coffin was prepared. Friends and relations kept coming to the house at all hours and we welcomed them as was customary, with tay and bread, pipe tobaccy and poitin.

Paul's Mary took care of all the arrangements. My job was to sit in the upper room next to Paddy and accept the kind words of those who arrived. Since our bedroom was just next to the upper room where Paddy was laid out, Mary would send me upstairs to the weans room to have a wee rest when I appeared tired.

Over the two days of the wake my rosary was never in its usual place hanging on the wall next to the St. Brigid's cross. It was to be found either in my hands or in someone else's, and every so often one of the family would lead us all in a decade of the rosary.

Sometimes my mind wanders when I say the rosary. I mind when I was wee, Father William McCafferty, our Parish Priest, scolding me and telling me that I should be prayerfully meditating upon the mysteries of faith.

It was before my First Communion, and I was kneeling in the chapel next to Mammy. I remember him standing there so tall and imposing, in his long black robe, his stern face turned toward me, shaking his finger rhythmically as he spoke, "Traditionally, reciting the Rosary means praying the full five decades while meditating on a particular mystery of faith. These mysteries are organised into three groups that are tied to certain days of the week. The "Joyful Mysteries" are recited on Mondays and Saturdays, the "Sorrowful Mysteries" are recited on Tuesdays and Fridays, the "Glorious Mysteries" are recited on Wednesdays and Sundays. What day is it wee Mary?"

I was so overcome that I could not mind the day. No answer came. Of course it was Sunday, that is the day we went to the chapel for Mass, but I could not speak. I was so shy and in awe of the Priest.

"See that you remember, wee Mary, see that you remember," he said, as he continued to the front of the chapel and into his chamber to prepare for the celebration of the Mass.

The set pattern of the Rosary has always been a comfort to me, especially "The Ave Maria" or "Hail Mary" prayer as it reminds me of the Blessed Virgin, Our Lady. Although when formally reciting the Rosary we say the prayers in Latin, when I am on my own, I pray in English.

Hail Mary, full of grace,
the Lord is with thee;
blessed are you among women,
and blessed is the fruit of thy womb.
Holy Mary, Mother of God,
pray for us sinners now
and at the hour of our death.

Normally I prefer the "Joyful Mysteries", even if it is not the right day. But during the wake, I found comfort in the "Sorrowful Mysteries." I could not see any joy in front of me at all.

It seemed I was saying the same things to everyone who came to the wake,

"Yes, he will be missed."

"Oh, he did have a good long life."

"Other than the blindness, he was very healthy."

"What a blessing that he passed so quickly and did not suffer."

These are the very same words that I had said myself to others before, in other homes, at other wakes, only this time it was my Paddy who was gone. My Paddy who would not be there that evening to discuss who had been at the corpse-house. My Paddy who would not be there to share in the gossip of the neighbourhood. The words might have been the same, but the day was so different. I found meself wanting to turn to him and share a story or a secret smile. I wondered if I would ever laugh again.

Our Curate, Father Daniel Reid, came up on Monday evening to pay his respects. He is a kind man who has worked in

5

the parish for some time now. He probably will become Parish Priest some day. He mentioned to Paul that the Parish Priest would come up to the house the next evening to go over all the arrangements for the funeral.

Our Parish Priest Father Philip O'Doherty did come up on Tuesday evening. He arrived with great pomp and ceremony. There is such a spirit about him that he seemed to fill the entire space of our upper room.

"The remains," he said, "should be prepared to leave the house by half ten. The pall-bearers will carry the coffin down Ballyloskey Road to the chapel with the funeral following behind. The mass will begin about 11 o'clock with the burial just afterward in the graveyard. Does that sound all right to ye"?

I wanted to shout that there was nothing all right about any of this, but I just nodded while Paul shook his hand and thanked him for coming. Many times in the past, I have noticed the grieving widows in the front of the chapel, flanked by their sons.

I never understood until now how much you can lean on the strength of your children when you do not feel like you can stand on your own.

Everyone said the funeral mass was beautiful. I agreed with them, of course, although I do not seem to mind any details from the mass. The weather was so very cold and blustery as we walked down to the chapel, the rain soaking my hat and coat.

The chapel was already filled with people and I do remember the smell of incense as we entered the chapel doors following the coffin. As was custom, I stopped at the Holy Water receptacle just inside the doors. Leaning my left hand on the cold stone wall for strength, and dipping my finger in the water, I made the sign of the cross with my right hand. The temperature of the water, normally a shock to my hand and head, barely registered. I walked numbly up the aisle toward the altar rail.

They set Paddy down at the front of the chapel and the Priest directed me to sit in the front pew to the left. I do not mind ever sitting so close to the altar before. The pews at the front of the chapel with the doors on the sides were reserved for the benefactors who had paid money to the church.

We always sat at the back, the women on the left side, the men on the right. I know that during the mass, my son Paul was on one side of me and my brother-in-law Willie Marley on the other. I do mind sitting there at the front of the church thinking that it had been many long years since I had Paul by my side for mass.

The last time was just after his First Communion. Paul still sat with the girls and me until one Sunday, Paddy's brother, Big Shan, stopped in the aisle just beside us, leaning across me, he whispered to Paul, "I see that you are still sitting with the women."

He then walked up a few rows, genuflected and went into his seat on the right. I remember that Paul hunched himself forward, grabbed his hat, and without looking me in the eye, quickly joined his uncle on the other side. That was the last time Paul was by my side until during Paddy's mass.

It was about a year later in the spring, after many a Sunday of looking longingly across the chapel at his older brother Paul, Eugene left me. He joined the men on the right side, even though he was still a couple of years shy of his First Communion.

From the time of my First Communion so long ago, I have always enjoyed looking towards the front of our chapel which was built in 1826. But during Paddy's mass, I wanted to look everywhere else except at the pine box set on the supports in the middle of the chapel.

The beautiful ornately carved wood that made up our altar and sacristy always commands my attention. I think that it is the perfect combination of ornate decoration that inspires worship and functional simplicity of design that inspires humility. That lovely altar was the centerpiece of our worship. The white linen cloth covering, which symbolizes purity of thought and action, was the perfect backdrop for the Priest to offer up the mystery of the Mass.

7

During Paddy's Mass, my mind wandered. I tried to imagine what it had been like before our chapel was built, during the time a Priest could be killed for celebrating Mass. Mammy told me that during the Penal times, the people would gather at

The Mass Rock in the Ancient Oak Grove, Carndonagh

the Mass Rocks. These were local, specifically appointed places, usually in a wood or on a secluded remote hill, where the rock would become the altar.

People would gather for hours before the Priest was set to arrive. Mammy said that folks would always walk purposefully but not quickly enough to appear anxious. Even the weans knew not to disclose where and when the Mass was to be said. It was important not to travel in too large a group. It took much planning and forethought to bring our spiritual leaders to the people during that time. Lookouts were appointed to watch for danger and give a warning so everyone could flee if necessary. For most Catholics, it required sacrifice and thus strengthened our faith.

Under these extreme conditions, people were lucky if they were able to take communion every month or so, whereas we are able to attend Mass now as often as we desire. We are very blessed.

The Mass Rock that Mammy showed me is on the other side of Carndonagh, past the St. Patrick's cross, and on towards Ballyliffin a short distance. Surrounded by an old oak forest, it is completely secluded. Mammy said that over 300 people could gather there for the celebration of the Mass and the British soldiers never did discover them. Today, it is so peaceful and quiet there in the forest that it is hard to imagine those difficult times long ago.

We were taught from the time we were wee to appreciate and revere our chapel because we were truly blessed to have the freedom to gather and worship in the manner we believe is right.

In our chapel, the twelve stained glass windows were imported from Italy, but the fourteen Stations of the Cross were hand carved locally. I knew without looking that there were twenty-five rows of pews on each side of the chapel as well as seven rows of pews up in the balcony. I had counted them many times before.

During Paddy's Mass, I could not make myself look around at those who were attending, but I knew that if I did turn my head, I would see our families and loved ones, our friends and our neighbours. Everyone who cared for us was there, it should have been a comfort, yet I felt so alone without my Paddy.

I looked ahead at the statue on the right of the altar. It is Our Lady with her hands outstretched in love. The statue to the left of the altar is St. Joseph holding the Christ Child. The lamps hanging from the ceiling had all their candles lit and the gold door to the Holy of Holies behind the altar glinted in the flickering candle light.

Everything is always so clean and tidy, and nothing is ever out of place in the chapel. The three steps leading up to the altar from behind the altar rail seemed to draw my thoughts heavenward and, for a moment, I felt as if I knew that Paddy was up there with the angels, looking down on all of us gathered for his Funeral Mass. I knew that he was pleased that he could see again, since the blindness had plagued him for so long.

The next memory I have is of the men lowering him into the ground and removing the ropes from under his casket. Then, as was our tradition, people filed past me as I stood by his grave, grasping my hands as they told me how sorry they were for my loss. I kept looking out past the chapel to the Derry Road and wished that I could let it take me anywhere but where I was at that moment.

I do not mind how I had gotten from the chapel out into the graveyard. Afterward, up at the house, I was worried about this gap in my memory and confided this to my sister Maggie. She assured me that sometimes when we have a great shock, we do not always mind the details. She said that it might come back to me later after some time has passed and her words were a great comfort to me.

And so I lie here tonight remembering the many nights gone by. Those first nights of our passion awakening, slumber forgotten as we bonded our souls together. Later there were nights when, after caring for one of the children, I would quietly creep into the warmth next to him trying not to awaken him.

At the end of other nights I would awaken to the first light of dawn and feel his warmth still lingering on the bedclothes after he had left to tend some of the livestock. But tonight as the tears roll down my cheeks onto my pillow, I realise that there will never again be his warmth in our bed.

As the days go by, I will probably let the grandchildren take turns sleeping with Granny. It will be a treat for them. But for now, this night, I will remember as I lie here alone and await the dawn.

Chapter 2

I Write My Story
September 1929

I have decided that I will write the story my life.

Last week as I was cleaning out my knitting basket, I found the papers that I had written on at the time of Paddy's death, folded up in the bottom. Reading what I had written brought back the memories all fresh in my mind.

That was such a difficult time for me; almost 10 years have passed and time does soften the pain somehow. I got to thinking that perhaps some of my children or grandchildren will be interested in my story after I am gone. I am especially thinking about the weans out in Oregon whom I have never met.

Sitting here by the light of the fire, as I ponder my life of more than 80 years, my mind is full of so many memories. Some of them bring a smile to my face and others bring a tear to my eye. I canna possibly write about everything that happened in my life, but I do want to chronicle the highlights. I only hope that I can get it all down before it is my time to go.

So this morning at breakfast, I asked to go to town with Paul. When he went for the messages, I purchased a wee blank book from Doherty's, the newsagents. It is one of those that the children use at school and has a hard black cover on the outside with lined paper inside.

Mrs. Doherty at the shop assumed that the book was for one of Paul's younger boys: John, Vincey or Harry. I could not tell her the truth and so I just agreed with her. I am not sure why, but I have the book hidden along with a pen in my knitting basket next to the fire.

I have not told anyone of my project. As I sit here remembering the days long gone, and when no one is about, I will write down my memories.

Mary Doherty in 1903

12

Chapter 3

My Birth
Spring 1847

I was born in the middle of the Great Hunger. At the time, no one knew what a defining time the years of 1846-1848 would be to the people of Ireland. It was not until years afterward that this particular famine period was called The Famine or The Great Hunger.

Folks where I was born knew that the potato crop had failed again, but they pulled together and worked hard, so it was not as great a tragedy to us as it was to those in other parts of Ireland. Just north of our town, there is a special thatched cottage alongside the Malin road called the Brachán House. Brachán is cooked corn gruel. In Ireland, corn is a general term for grains and cereal crops, typically oats. From 1846 to 1849 there was a very large pot of meal cooked everyday at the Brachán House to feed anyone who had a need. Maize or Indian Corn, imported from America, was difficult to grind in our local mills. It did not gain popularity as cattle feedstuff until later.

The meal was supplied by the Clonmany and Donagh Relief Committee. The government had organised these local relief committees in an effort to encourage local responsibility in relieving those in need. People would walk for miles, if they were destitute, to receive a ladle full of gruel in their cup. The meal was portioned out based on the number of people in each house. The daily ration consisted either of one pound of meal (ground flour or grain) or one quart of soup thickened with a portion of meal. Children below the age of nine were allotted half rations.

The townland of Ballyloskey where I was born is a mile outside the town of Carn. Officially on the map, the town is listed as Carndonagh, but everyone calls it Carn. Located in the middle of the Inishowen Peninsula in our lovely county of Donegal, Carn is the area's market town.

Our road, the Ballyloskey Road, begins just down on the Derry Road a little ways off from the Workhouse. Ballyloskey means "townland of fire." It probably was so named because of the ancient lime kilns in Upper Ballyloskey. The smoke from the kilns could be seen for miles and did look as if the townland was on fire.

The road winds up into the rolling Donegal hills and ends in the bog fields of the area called Upper Ballyloskey. Our house was about half way up, where the road takes a sharp turn to the right past our front door and around the back of the house.

On a clear day, I could sit on our front door step and, turning my head from the left to right, see past Slieve Snacht (the Snowy Mountain) all the way to Glentogher, straight out Trawbreaga Bay to the Isle of Doagh and on to Knockamany Bends. Over to the right was just a bit of a view of Culdaff Bay. Some days though, if the weather was bad, I could barely see Fanny Canny's field in front of the house.

My father always said that my birth occurred during the lambing of 1847. It had been seven years since Mammy had carried a child to term. Out in the field behind our house, while assisting the ewes birthing the lambs, he was worried that whole day and night as Mammy was birthin' me in the cottage.

He remembered that it was bitter cold and he was not only worried about losing some ewes and lambs that night, but he was worried about losing Mammy and me. Granny Kate was helping, along with my two aunties and the handy-woman, Margaret Callahan.

Everyone was relieved when my puny cry broke the silence of the dawn. They say that I was scrawny but strong. I guess that describes me still. As a wean, my hair was very light, almost colourless and as I grew older, it darkened into a heathery brown colour.

Every summer my hair would lighten with the sun and then be darker for the winter. My father said that my eyes never changed colour from the first time I looked up at him. He often told me that in them he saw the colour of a summer sky.

As is traditional, they named me Mary after my father's mammy, Granny Mary. She was Mary married to Hugh Doherty. No one minds her maiden name anymore. Her husband was Hugh and when they married she was called Mary Hudie.

Because practically everyone around here is Doherty or McLaughlin, with the way of Irish nicknames, we are known as the Hudies. I am wee Mary Hudie although my proper name is Mary Doherty. Even after my marriage to Big Paddy Newman, whose proper name is Patrick Doherty, I was still called wee Mary Hudie.

It can be confusing as there are no set rules to nicknames. Although we are Dohertys, those in our house are known as the Hudies, except my father. He is known as John Shoemaker because he is the shoemaker. Johnny Tailor lives up the hill and John Cloth is over the fields. You can guess what they do for work.

Nicknames can also be given for a physical feature or for where you live. You can have known someone your whole life and unless you attend their wedding or the baptism of their child or even their funeral, you may never know their proper surname.

My father came from down by Quigley's Point. It is about ten miles from where I was born. He had come up to Carn on a Fair Day and had seen my mother. He often told us weans that he could never forget her, so he had to marry her. We would all laugh at the thought of our parents falling in love.

It is customary for the sons to retain the lease on the land, but Mammy was the last one of her house left at home. Her older brother and sister had already left home for Boston. So after my parents were married, my granda asked my father to take over his lease. Granda decided that my parents would raise their family in my mammy's homeplace.

Eventually, there were eight of us reared in the house. Our Paddy was born first. I was seven years younger. Hugh was born the year I started school. Philip and Sadie came along within a few years of Hugh. John and Maggie came along when I was a teenager. I was eighteen by the time Wee Patrick arrived. He was born a few years after my older brother Paddy died out in America and so the new baby was named after him, to honour him, as was customary.

A few others were born to Mammy in between all of us, but they did not live long. Some other babies were expected for a while, but they never were born. Although she would stop and say the rosary, she never would talk about those white crosses marking the small graves outside the walls of the graveyard. The unbaptised babies could not be buried in consecrated ground.

Out in Straths, on the way to Ballyliffin, in the townland of Carndoagh, there is a separate burial ground for unbaptised weans, but at our chapel, they are buried outside the walls.

I did not understand Mammy's silence until I too had to stand by a grave and watch the shovelfuls of dirt fall on a small blanket covered body and know that never again would I see a smile light up the face of my beloved baby. My face stoic, and outwardly calm, my eyes brimming with unshed tears, I then understood my mother's pain.

Through a child's eyes, however, I had not understood the world of the adults that surrounded me.

As a child, my world was the fields and lanes, the ditches and the hedges that began just at the end of our garden. My earliest recollection is chasing butterflies across the road and into Canny's field. I must have been about four or five years old.

I had finished all my chores, the bedclothes had been tidied, the potatoes and turnips scrubbed for the pot, the cow was milked.

Finally Mammy said, "Go for a wee walk, head on up to McLaughlin's and see if your friends are out. Enjoy yourself."

The McLaughlin girls that lived at the top of the brae, across from the Newmans, were my best friends. Sicily and Elizabeth were both older than me, with Kate a year younger. When permitted, the four of us were always in each others' company.

I pulled on a jumper and scampered out the door into the spring sunshine. Barely warm, the sun had chased away the chill. There was no bitter wind that usually was so common. The five minute walk up to McLaughlin's passed pleasantly and in no time I was down their street and at their front door. The half door was open, but when I peered in, there was no one at home. I called out to my friends, but there was no answer. Disappointed, I began trudging the long walk back home. The day seemed suddenly dreary, as I no longer felt the light-hearted anticipation of seeing my friends.

Halfway down the hill, I heard birds chirping cheerfully from behind the ditch. Although their song seemed to mock my mood, it drew me towards them. I looked around and saw no one so I cautiously ventured forth.

Crossing the road, I saw the open gate and peered around the bushes into the field. Then I saw the butterfly. Playfully dancing in the air, it teased me to follow. I could not resist. My spirits lifted, we danced the age old dance of children and nature. I do not know how long I played or when Mammy called me in, but the memory of that moment in time is strong.

And in those dark moments that come to each of us over a lifetime, when the way is hard and there is no apparent joy to be seen, sometimes, if I let meself, I can still see the butterfly and suddenly I am back again, four years old, flitting around Canny's field laughing with the butterflies.

I enjoyed working with Mammy. She often told me how much she counted on me as we worked side by side. Having reared my own children, I now know how much help I actually was, but at the time, all I knew was that she counted on me.

From the time I can remember, it was my job first thing in the morning to fill up the turf bin next to the fire. I would open the heavy door to the outside and walk along the footpath to the turf shed. As I grew older the path seemed to grow shorter, but as a young child, it was a great journey.

Mammy and my father would laugh between themselves as I solemnly fulfilled my duty. I knew, as they had often told me, that the entire house would be cold if I neglected to bring in the turf each morning. It was miraculous to me every morning that, by carefully placing a couple pieces of turf and blowing a few breaths on the ashes from last night's fire, Mammy would quickly have the warm earthy smell wafting through the room as the smoke curled up the chimney. I often think of her still as I re-light the fire each morning at my own hearth.

Every few days, I was allowed to scrape out the ashes that had fallen below the grate on the hearth and take them out back to the ash pile. This, too, was an important job because the ash was essential to soap-making and my father would plow it into certain fields that were not producing as well as he would like.

Mammy and I prepared the breakfast table after the fire was started. Many a morning, the great pot of oatmeal was re-warmed over the fire. Eaten with buttermilk from our milk cow, it was a grand meal, or so said my father. And we believed him. If there was no oatmeal, we would have spuds with the buttermilk.

Our Paddy and my father would leave to work in the fields after breakfast. For many years it was a great mystery to me what they did all day long. My duties kept me in the house with Mammy while Paddy headed out each day doing mens' work. He would fall into his bed after his tea, exhausted. It seemed like a great adventure. I longed to join them in that adventure.

After breakfast, Mammy would turn her thoughts to the dinner. There were always potatoes; late summer and autumn we had carrots or turnips. Mammy would make a scone with her flour and sometimes there were a few eggs if the hens were laying. It was simple fare, but we were never hungry and there always seemed to be enough. My parents worked hard to provide for our family. Some families did not weather the farming ups and downs as well as we did.

Although there are no stories of starvation in our house, the story is told locally of seven people lying dead along Ballyloskey Road during the Great Hunger, with green stains circling their emaciated mouths. It is said that they were too proud to stand in line at the Brachán House with a cup in their outstretched hand. Instead, they had tried to eat grass to stave off their hunger.

Chapter 4

Good Times Begin
Autumn 1851

I do not recall my earliest memory of my husband Paddy Newman. It seems that he has always been in my life. He was one of "the Newmans", the family that lived at the top of the brae, just opposite the McLaughlins. They were Dohertys, but like us they were always called by their nickname. They had six of a family: Big Shan was the eldest, followed by the four girls, Kate, Rosie, Mary and Nellie. Paddy was the last. Nine years older than me, it seems that Paddy was always part of my life, when I was an infant, a toddler and later a schoolgirl.

The thing that I mind most about him when I was young is that he was my brother Paddy's best friend. Typical young boys, the two Paddys were always teasing me, or poking me just to get me riled up. I would run from them screaming, and then later sneak up through the fields to Newman's just to see what was on up there.

To me, life was more exciting around the two boys. There was always a crinkle of a smile about Paddy Newman's face when he would look at me. It was as if he knew a secret that I did not know. Later he told me that he had watched and waited for me to grow up. I do not know about that; it would be another story.

But I do mind a time before I started school. I was probably four years old or somewhere close to it. I was out at the edge of the field watching the men help my father turn the hay. The pitch forks were thrust into the dried hay and although the men were sweating, it seemed as if the hay effortlessly floated into the air and turned over onto itself to dry the other side. They were laughing and talking as men do, hardly noticing the work they were doing.

I remember watching Paddy standing in the heat of the summer sun. He would have only been about thirteen years old, although he was already tall. They were calling him Big Paddy even then. I think that he grew to be over six feet tall. I do not know how tall for sure, for we never measured him. Even in his stooped old age he would tower over most men. He had big strong shoulders and thick strong arms.

I suppose that day of haying was the first time I especially noticed Big Paddy Newman.

I remember that he remarked that it was a good harvest and he hoped that the rains would not come too soon to spoil it. He also said that he was grateful for such good weather. I remember feeling excitement and hope from the men. It was palpable. It must be remembered that there had not been that feeling in my short lifetime, for I was born in the middle of the Great Hunger. That harvest of 1851was anticipated as being the first good crop in many years. There was no fear of famine that summer. That lack of fear left a void in our lives and hope began to trickle in to fill it.

Our lives were spent so close to the land and the seasons that it is difficult to explain the thoughts and fears of the local people of that time to someone who did not experience it. Although the famine times had not been as tragic in our area as in other parts of Ireland, we had heard the stories from the travelling people and the clergy.

The horrors of West Donegal and Galway were told and re-told over the ditches and doorways. The fear of the Great Hunger coming again hung over us all. Every spring planting brought with it the worry of whether there would be a harvest. Even when the green shoots pushed through the soil and began to leaf, there was the fear of the blight.

For years after, the men would hesitate to turn the praties at the beginning of the harvest, in case they would again discover the black mush instead of firm brown potatoes. They remembered how it seemed as if the plants had withered and the praties dissolved before their very eyes. The blight which began in 1846 had taken everyone by surprise. At first the plants looked strong and healthy, but as that summer went on a strange foul vapour arose from the fields. No one had ever smelt it before but it became a well known feature during those years. The smell seemed to emanate from the decaying stalks, filling the air with the malignant odour. No one who had smelt the horrible stench ever forgot.

As the seasons passed and years turned by with crops not failing and blight not coming, we all seemed to release the collective breath that we had been holding. Some playfulness re-entered our lives as we began to move some of the dreariness aside.

New ideas about animal husbandry were being discussed among the men. The turnip root had been introduced as a source of winter feedstuff. This was causing the cattle trade to increase. It was now possible to select and breed cattle, keeping them from year to year, instead of killing them off annually. Indian corn was promoted as being good fodder for cattle and the local mills were able to supply the farmers with more variety in feedstuffs. I heard the older ones remark that times were going to be different. It was spoken in such a hopeful way.

We children did not know any different, but with the faith that children have in their parents' reassuring words, we knew that the hard times were now past and the rainbow was around the corner. Life was precious and fragile and our time was spent working and preparing to sustain that life.

It was expected that once you reached the age of twelve that formal school was finished and you worked the land. Everyone keenly felt the responsibility of working to support the family. It was difficult for families to get the money together to pay the rent to the landlord and feed everyone.

Some small-holding farmers had to send their children and teenagers to the hiring fairs to be hired out. The hiring fairs had developed from the need for farmer and labourer to find a common place to meet and strike a bargain for the work time period and wages. It became common for specific fair days to be called hiring fairs.

These hiring fairs were usually held twice a year, in May and November, although some towns had hiring fairs all on their own not connected to the ordinary fair day. The main hiring fairs in our area were held in the Diamond in Derry City and Letterkenny, but there were some children hired out from our Carn Fair. The farmer would strike a bargain with the father and then children would leave with the farmer for six months or a year, whatever was the agreed term. They would be fed and have shelter in the barn and were expected to work fourteen to sixteen hours a day. The full work day was supposed to be 13 hours with two or three one-hour breaks.

That was not always the norm. If a worker left before the term was up, they forfeited whatever wages had been earned. A child's reputation would be tarnished and other farmers would hear about his attitude and he would not be given another term. Times were tough and money was scarce, so most workers stayed for the full term no matter what the conditions were.

Some bigger towns started having a runaway hiring fair held the day after the usual hiring fair. Here escapees were allowed a chance to find a second master for the term.

The first farm season from May to November would be spent mostly outdoors. In addition to helping with the harvest and picking potatoes, children would be expected to tend the livestock, milk the cows in the morning and evening, churn butter and gather eggs. Meadowlands were cleared of stones and other obstructions that might hinder reaping and fences were repaired to keep wandering animals out. The turf would be brought from the bog and stored in the turf shed. Roof repair and thatching would be completed.

The second farming season from November to May would be spent repairing and preparing. Land needed for planting would be drained and ploughed, ditches and drains were cleared, sloughs were drained, walls rebuilt and boundary hedges repaired. Girls would be taught to twist hay or straw into ropes and help with the washing and cooking.

Workers would be expected to work six days a week and sometimes most of the seventh. In the spring and summer the day would start around six in the morning and go until dusk, which could be 17 hours later. More workers were taken for the first term than the second because of the heavy summer workload.

At the end of each term, the father would travel to the farm to collect his children and receive the wages from the farmer. The money was used to pay the family obligations, such as tithes to the established church until 1839, and the ever oppressive land rent. Some farmers would make deductions from the wages for clothes, boots, pocket money or broken articles. Sometimes, if the child was unlucky and the farmer kept a careful record, the wages would be whittled away on frivolity, so that at the end of the term there was not much money to be handed over to the father.

Some people thought that hired workers were short-changed, but they did get their meals and board included as part of the hiring arrangement. The workers had the security of a contract and were not subject to layoffs and interruptions. There was a wide variation in living conditions. Some lived in deplorable conditions and others lived on par with their employers.

In winter things were particularly harsh. Out buildings, like the barns, would be freezing with icicles around the walls and wind whistling through the rafters above. Sometimes the weans beds were nothing more than a blanket thrown over some straw on the floor. It was a hard life. Lucky for us none of our people had to be hired out. Some of the young people used this time of hiring to learn skills that were sound preparation for travelling to Scotland as a young adult when they would hire out for seasonal agricultural work across the sea.

My next specific memory of Paddy might have been that same summer or it could have been the one following. I do not know which year it was, but school was finished for the boys and they were now out working with the men. Kate McLaughlin and I were sitting just inside the garden next to the stone wall, playing in the dirt, making little houses of stones. We were pretending and fantasising as young girls do. One little stone was me and another was my husband. A group of stones were all my children. Kate had her family of stones around her. Other stones were the house, the byre and the barn. I had my whole life played out in front of me with my wee stone garden.

Paddy jumped himself up onto the stone wall and laughed out loud. He said that although I was wee, my biggest strength was that I had everything organised into its proper place. I knew how everything would work out and what everyone would do and how it would all be.

His words did not sound like a compliment to me.

I stood up and yelled at him, "I am going to marry you Big Paddy Newman, just you wait and see. This is you. You are this stone."

He laughed at me and jumped off the wall into the garden.

My brother Paddy, who of course was sitting right next to Big Paddy, since they were inseparable, jumped down into the middle of my stone world and kicked it all apart. I screamed and ran into the house, to receive some comfort from Mammy. I wanted to discuss the injustice of older brothers, I wanted retribution, I wanted...., well, I wanted our Paddy to be in trouble.

As I was running to the house, I did hear Big Paddy scolding our Paddy.

"Paddy ye should not torture her like that. What has she done to deserve that? She is just a wee girl and was not hurting anyone with her dreams and her plans."

He then told our Paddy that he was just being cruel. Big Paddy had defended me even to my own brother, and that meant something to me.

Chapter 5

My Childhood

I mind the time I finally was allowed to go with the boys into the fields. I had just made my First Communion earlier that spring. It was hay time. The famine was over and emigration had hit our community hard. There were no labourers to hire. The young ones had left their own hearths and homes to find work in England, America or Australia.

Daddy and Mammy had a huge row. Paddy, Hugh and I were quiet in our trundle bed, just below them on the floor, pretending to be asleep.

Mammy said, "Mr. Doherty, 'tis not right for our Mary to have to go out into the fields. She is too young. The work will be too hard for her and then she will be in your way and you will be cross with her."

My father was silent for a few moments. I thought that he had fallen asleep.

Finally he just said, "Kate, ye can get along well enough without her for one day, I need the wean."

I thought of my friends from school, most of the other children my age, both boys and girls, had already experienced that great excitement of heading out to work with their fathers.

I wanted to shout out, "I am strong, I can do it. Even my friend Kate who is younger has missed some days of school to help with the haying."

But I was afeared of letting them know that I was still awake. I drifted off to sleep not knowing my fate.

In the morning, Mammy did not say a word as father gruffly spoke to me, "Wee Mary, find your brógaí and pull on your warm jumper. Leave your school books to the side. Ye are headin' to the fields with me today."

I was so excited that it took me too long to find the brógaí, which were just outside the door where I had left them. Paddy and Daddy were out the door and away down the lane when I came limping and jumping along behind them.

Calling out to them to wait for me, I was trying to get the brógaí on my feet at the same time as I was pulling the jumper down over my head. I must have been a sight. Our Paddy was doubled over with laughter and I saw the twinkle in my father's eye as he was growling at me to hurry along.

It was exciting to learn how to turn the still wet hay in the field. I watched the men expertly roll the hay into sheaves and throw them into the stacks. Try as I might, it was a skill that I would never master.

The work of sustaining life was the same day to day in every cottage. After waking in the morning, everyone would straighten up their sleeping space, whether it was the day bed or a trundle. The woman of the house would stir about the coals of the turf fire from the day before to restore the blaze in the fireplace and begin cooking the morning meal. The time in between food preparation was filled with cleaning and repairing our homes and working the fields. It was how we all survived.

Entertainment was of our own making, telling stories or singing songs. Often it was the bright spot in what could be a monotonous, dreary existence. The work was often interrupted by conversations with others. Neighbours would walk by or relations would call. We would sit around talking about each other, discussing who did what to whom and why.

Such common titbits as a baby coming too early or too late, an old granny finally taking her last breath after a long struggle, or early frost on the hills could occupy our conversations for days. We were known to discuss not only what had happened, but also what was going to happen, what was expected to happen and what actually never did happen.

The main topic to be commonly discussed was the weather. It played a central role in our lives and so we talked about it. What the weather had been, what it was going to be, what we could do if only it was different. Nothing that happened in our own little community seemed very shocking when compared to the events on the world level. We learned about the world through the weekly newspapers we shared with one another. These topics also consumed our thoughts and conversations.

From the time I was a wean, my Mammy would say, "today's actions create tomorrow's results." It would make me think of what I wanted tomorrow to look like.

If we went to bed at night and did not bank the coals properly, the fire would be difficult or almost impossible to start in the morning. It could take an extra hour of time as well as a lot of extra pieces of bogwood and turf to get the fire rebuilt for cooking and that would waste our scant resources.

So at night the precautions taken with the coals of the fire were in preparation for the morrow. If the praties were not stored properly they would not keep over the winter and then by March we would be hungry. If the meat was not salted and cured properly it too would not be preserved. The maggots would eat better than the family. If the hens were not fed, we would not have eggs. With all these things, Mammy taught me in a tangible way that you must think now, plan now, act now in order to have the outcome in the future that you desire and even need to survive. The weather was so changeable in our part of the world. The day could start out clear and you could have three or four different weather changes before mid-day. Fog was something we could have in any season. Sometimes during the summer, the fog would rise up out of the ground in the morning, even if the sky was clear, especially if the air had been moist the day before and not particularly dry. This ground fog would be in a layer rising from the earth, especially at sunrise. Then the pink sky of sunrise from the east would appear to chase away the grey mass of the fog in the west. This summer fog would disappear as the day brightened and you would know that the day would be dry.

Local farmers would help one another, especially during the harvest time by taking in the corn, and turning the hay or digging the praties. All the men in our area would gather one day at one farm and then the next at another, wherever the help was needed. Each family was benefitting from and serving each other in turn. It was expected that everyone would gather together to get all the crops in.

The corn, or grain, was cut by bending over it, grasping a bunch of straw in the left hand, inserting the hook of the sickle and drawing it toward the body in a sawing action. It was important to cut low to the earth and be gentle so that none of the precious grain was lost or damaged. It was back breaking work. Each man gathered the loghters, or armfuls of grain. The loghters were bound into sheaves, and then a few more men came along behind placing the sheaves into stooks.

At harvest time, you would see a line of men bending and stooping each one working their different job with the grain, and at the end of the line would be the stooks. From a distance it almost looked as if they magically appeared at the end of the work line.

The autumn feast, or Meitheal, was the party at the end of the harvest. The word meitheal was an Irish word that means a gang of workmen working together to harvest any crop. But it also came to mean the important celebration of prosperity after the hard work was over. There was music and great craic altogether. Everyone looked forward to the feast.

Chapter 6

Cutting Turf

he weather could be so damp that sometimes I would not feel that I had been warm for months. Winters were harsh with the cold wind coming off the North Atlantic that cut right through your clothes and chilled your bones. The only heat in the house came from the turf fire. Turf was our only fuel for cooking and heating. With it we sustained our lives.

There was plenty of turf to be had in the bog, but it was back-breaking work to harvest, dry and haul it down to the turf shed beside the house. Typically the men and boys would go up into the bog for a couple of days each week beginning in the spring. Working the turf always began in the middle of March after lambing and spring planting because the bog was wetter and much easier to work.

Bringing in the turf was a three or four man job. It was a right auld walk up into the bog before they started work at all. I mind my father doing the ritting by creating a line cutting down through the sod followed by the flactering, which was peeling the sod back to expose the turf. It was always exciting to see the rich dark turf emerge from under the grass.

The bog with turf was covered by long coarse grass and small shrubs. It is indistinguishable from heather and other swampy land. I remember asking my father how he knew where to find good turf.

He said, "Wee Mary, ye canna tell from the top surface of the land whether the area will have peat moss suitable for turf or not. There are areas of the bog where there is no turf on at all. Ye just have to know."

"Your granda took me up to the fields with him when I was wee and solemnly showed me our turf bank. I will never forgit that day. He said that this wee strip of land was given to us by God in Heaven to sustain us. Working the bank right would keep our family for as long as we needed it."

It is important not to over harvest a bank.

My father often remarked, "We canna be greedy, we only take what we need from the bank. We cut along the face until we have enough and leave it. When we return the next spring, it is waiting for us to begin where we left off."

Some banks have been harvested for generations. It is easy to spot them out in the bog. They have a wall measuring six or eight feet from the sod down to the bottom of the channel.

Creating a new turf bank was hard going. The first step was to dig a two foot wide trench by hand. Cutting down through the sod, the men would create a face down the length of the bank. This work was done over the winter. On dryer days when there was not much other work to do around the farm the men would head up to the bog to work the new bank. This preparation made it ready to harvest the following spring.

The depth of turf in a bank varies. The turf can be anywhere from a foot deep to more than 20 feet deep. Sometimes a bank is left alone by a family for a few years to let it regenerate and then the harvest begins again.

Every family would have its own banks that would be worked in pairs. Keeping them going in pairs was called the pairing. The bank would be cut about six turf wide which is about two foot six inches. Then, with the turf spade, they would peel back the top layer of the bog to expose the turf, the peat moss, beneath. The sod would be kept lying on top of the peat moss to protect the turf until there was no chance of frost.

Our Turf Bank in Meenahuner before the harvest.

Out where we cut turf in Meenahuner (which means the grey rock), our bank is over 300 yards long. At the end it goes down to a swamp where there is no turf. The top layer is soft brown in colour and the under-layer as black as coal. This under-layer is much better turf. The first 200 yards of our bank is two turf deep. This means that after the top layer of vegetation, you can cut two turf lengths with the spade until you hit the hard rock bottom called the channel. The further down into the bog you go, away from the road, our bank becomes three and then four turf deep. At the end of our bank, before the swamp, you can cut down 20 feet deep and still not hit the channel.

Depending on the weather, the men would return to the bog a couple of weeks after the ritting and flactering to cut the turf. If a heavy frost came on after the turf was cut and laid out to begin drying, it would destroy it. Weather was the determining factor for when to cut the turf.

The turf spade had a back on it and a lug on the side that cut out the shape of the turf. The length of the cut turf log would depend on the particular bank: they might be two foot six down to eighteen inches long, but they were on average about two feet in length. The man cutting the turf down in the hole was called the holer. He would cut the turf and throw it out to the man on the bank. The man on the bank would throw the turf further back onto the spread field so they would dry.

Two days of cutting would fill 20 to 25 cartloads which was enough turf to keep a family through the winter. Then there was the day for pairing, then the work of turning, footing and dragging before you hauled the turf home.

During some years we had an early spring of fine weather and then the weather would suddenly turn. In those years we would have an easier time getting our turf if we brought it in early, in other years it was better to wait.

Sometimes if the weather turned really harsh in the spring and early summer, loads of turf would be seen lying beside the road in the bog, ruined because they had not been brought in soon enough. The men always counted on a bit of luck to choose the time to harvest the turf. To cut the turf, the turf spade would be used to chop off blocks of the soggy vegetation. The blocks or logs would be laid out on top of the bog to begin the draining process. The men would split their time between cutting new blocks and turning the other ones. The turf logs would be turned over every few days until they were deemed sufficiently dry to foot.

If there was a week's good weather the turf would be ready for footing. Footing the turf was done by placing one block flat on the ground and standing another block alongside of it with a fairly good slope. Then the rest of the turf logs would be placed standing up leaning on one another, similar to the Indian tee-pee frames of America.

Depending on the size of the logs cut, each footing would have between four to seven turf logs. The main reason to foot the

Footing the Turf in Meenahuner

turf with them standing up was so wind could go through them and the sun would dry them out.

A week or so later the turf would be turned around, sometimes two footings would be combined into one. This was called second footing. It often turned into a game of speed and skill between the neighbours to see who could foot the most turf in the day.

Turf from other bogs that were good and flat would never need footing, the men could get away with just turning them over twice, but in the bogs up in the hills, the turf always needed footing. Turf from some of the wetter banks would require a second footing to completely dry. It might be another couple of weeks before they were ready for the dragging. The turf would be taken from the footings in the bog and stacked up next to the hard road.

Before we had a horse, my Paddy would use a wheelbarrow to do the dragging. It was tough going. Since getting the horse, it was a little easier. He used a slipe, a horse-drawn flat bed on runners to move the turf. The men threw the turf on the flat bed and the horse drug it up to the road for stacking. It is only possible to drag turf when the weather is good.

If the weather got bad before the dragging, the men had to go into the bog and hand carry the turf out in bags or put them into baskets on a donkey. A horse was no use, it would get stuck in the mire. But if the weather was great, the stacks would sit there for another two or three weeks getting more season on them before they were taken in to the turf shed or to put on the stack outside the back door. The more seasoned they were, the easier handled because they were lighter, with less water in them. The old ones always say that the turf is better seasoned in the bog than in the shed.

The weather for cutting is usually dampish thus the sod is dripping wet. It is like cutting out big clumps of black clay. When it dries out, the sod becomes the turf that we know, the crackly, dried out fibrous matter. It cracks and flakes and becomes powdery and dusty and everyone is covered in the dust. The dust cakes your eyelashes, goes into your ears and gets stuck in your teeth. The weather for the footing was drier and if all went well, the turf was well dried out for the dragging, stacking and carting back home.

That time of year the black flies and midgies would be out. They seemed to know if someone was new to bringing in the turf and it was as if they thought they could eat the visitor alive. Between the dust and the bugs, many hated the hill, but there were those who loved the time of bringing in the turf. The stories of long days of summer sunshine and the craic, the hard work and the camaraderie were told and retold all winter long.

The weans would remember jumping from the top of one bank to the next, and again laugh at the unfortunate one who had missed jumping all the way to the next bank and had fallen down into the murky black pools that formed at the bottom of the cutting. One danger that we all knew to avoid was the smooth areas in the middle of the banks that were covered with grass. Even though the cut turf drying on top of the mossy grass was full of dust, the uncut bog was full of water.

Sometimes this mossy grass was the deceptive covering for sink holes of water-logged peat moss and dust. If you stepped on a grass covered sink hole, instead of on terra firma, you would immediately begin to sink into the freezing cold water. The sinking one would have to be pulled back out by others.

The waterlogged bog created a suction on the person, so strong that they would lose shoes or other pieces of clothing as they were pulled out, depending on how far down in the sink hole they had gone. There was no retrieving those lost articles.

The clothes that did come out with the victim were mingin', dirty and stained brown from the bog water. They would be washed and repaired but would remain a reminder of a tragedy averted, so even the youngest child knew to jump from bank to bank and avoid the dangerous part down in the middle.

In a couple of weeks, the stacks were ready to load into the cart to be taken back to the house. If one had a donkey, this was easier; otherwise the men would pull the cart home themselves. Load by load the men would stack the turf in the turf shed next to the house. This process seemed to take all summer. If there were relations home visiting we could get all the cousins to go up the hill and help with footing the turf.

Out at Meenahuner, there is a great view of Trawbreaga Bay, Dunaff Head, Mamore Gap, to Carn and even the Derry Road. On a clear day you can see for miles. We would make a day of it and take our dinner with us.

My father would cut a hole in the turf for the basket of sandwiches and scone bread, with another for the bottle of tea and one for the bottle of milk. The food would stay cool in the sod until we were ready to eat it, even on the hottest summer's day.

Everywhere you looked you would see little tufts of smoke rising where each family would make a fire in the turf to boil the eggs and make the tea for the meal. We would all rest for fifteen minutes or so and then by some unspoken signal all were up and away at the work again. I mind one time when I was still wee being a bit tired of the working, so I began running in and around the area where the turf was footed. It was great craic.

It seems that I tossed the footings with me running around.

My father reared up on me, shouting, "Wee Mary, ye will have to put them all back as they were."

I was so frightened, I was shaking. I turned right away, bending up and down, trying to carefully replicate the footings as I had seen the men prepare them. I must have been a sight.

Behind my back, I heard the soft chuckle of my father. He noticed me quickly turn around, but I was just in time to see his big smile vanish as he straightened his mouth, wrinkling his brow, to wear his stern "disciplining the weans" expression. He stood stoic, smoking his pipe, watching me trying to repair the damage. Although he appeared angry at me, it was good training for when I would be bigger and my labour would be imperative to bringing in the turf for our family.

When it was finally time to bring the turf in, the pieces were stacked up 10 to 12 feet high on the cart, and the weans would sit up on top of the lot like kings on a throne as we led the horse, winding down the hill to the farm. Weans had the job of carrying the turf logs off the cart to the men stacking in the shed. Everyone worked together. If your family did not get your turf in, you would have a sad, cold winter.

During the spring and summer we would cut turf not only for ourselves, but after our marriage, Paddy and I also cut turf for paying our land rent as well as trading with the townspeople of Carn for goods from the shops. Some of those families just wanted Paddy to cut the turf and they would come up into the hill and foot it themselves. Paddy made arrangements with some of the families in the town to get them their turf and then we were able to trade that for flour and sugar, lamp oil and other staples.

One year early on, Maggie, the widow down the road, had a string of bad luck. She had a bad crop so she was short on money, and then a fox got into her hens and they all died, so then she had no eggs to sell. Then the next week her milk cow dried up, so that there was no butter either. The grocer said that she could have no more credit in the store until she had somehow paid the bill. I was in the shop the day that she got this bad news, and I went right home and told Paddy. So he got some of the other men in the townland and they all brought in some turf to settle her balance with the grocer.

She was never told who had exacted her deliverance, but there was a lightness in her step and a smile on her face for weeks afterward that was grand.

A lot of the bog land was held in commonage; no one owned it. That meant that each family had a right to harvest what they needed to sustain their family. Other banks were attached to a particular farm. No one took advantage of this, and in fact if one man needed less fuel than his neighbour and was finished bringing in his turf, he would join in with the rest, working the turf, until all had what they needed. It was hard work, but it was the way that our community made sure everyone had heat and fuel to cook with. This process has not changed here for hundreds of years.

Chapter 7

I Enjoy Walking

ne of my favourite places to walk with a dear friend or to spend some time pondering and thinking alone was down Ballyloskey, across the Derry Road to the path behind the Workhouse, and then along the river as it wandered through the landscape towards where it empties into Trawbreaga Bay. Up river it is called the Glentogher River as it winds through Glentogher and the name changes to the Donagh River as it approaches Carn.

Along the way, there are some wee rock-falls; not really big enough to call them water-falls. The branches from willow trees along the banks hang down and dance along the surface of the water. It is called a river, but compared to the mighty rivers that I had heard about in school, I think it is really more like a stream.

Each time I began my walk, the sounds from the Workhouse would fade rapidly and were replaced by the sounds of the wind and the birds. Once I came upon a badger. I do not know who was more startled, but we both fled in opposite directions and I never saw him again. On Market days, unless the breeze blows the other way, I could smell the Horse Market before I was actually along-side it. The stalls for the horses were just at the river's edge and I usually avoided taking my walks on those days. It was just not as pleasant.

Donagh River under Bridge Street Carndonagh

Just past the Horse Market there is a rock I enjoyed resting on below the bridge of Bridge Street in the town. The wind carries the sounds from the town, sounds of commerce and industry, the shirt factory as well as the shops nearby.

Sometimes I heard people stopping on the bridge greeting each other and sharing a bit of gossip. There are also those people who just talk to themselves. No one seemed to know that I was there listening to their lives.

The river meanders through the fields of Liss to the rocky beach of Trawbreaga Bay. The bay is a shallow saltwater inlet from the North Atlantic ocean, so when the tide is out there is much to explore on the seabed. I usually gathered seaweed that clung to the rocks and some mussels if I could find them. Dried seaweed or dulse is a local treat and most houses have some to offer to visitors and guests.

Trawbreaga is a haven for many varieties of birds: guillemots, water birds, swans, various gulls, oyster catchers and shell duck. The name Trawbreaga means 'lying strand' and has a mysterious history. Local stories say that a princely castle was at one time swallowed by the sea, and local boatmen say that at certain times in the year the chimney tops of this castle are still visible in the depths below. I never did see them.

At least once a week, I would find the time in the midst of my chores to take my walk. Even on a wet day it was pleasurable, although I had to be careful as the rain made the stones along the river slippery and I actually fell in a time or two. My parents knew that if ever it appeared that I had gone missing, they just needed to send someone down along the river towards Trawbreaga and there I would be found.

When I was about fifteen, I discovered another magical place in my wanderings. Instead of turning downstream at the Workhouse, I turned to the left and began to head upstream, away from Carn towards Glentogher. I do not know how long I walked that day and I never did measure how many miles, but I think that it must be at least five miles from the Workhouse. It is just beyond the place where the river crosses under the Derry road and slices into the hillside. A few hill sheep were meandering and I had followed them in their wanderings. I came upon some rocks and trees nestled together on the hillside and stopped to notice the sun glinting through the trees.

Suddenly a bit of movement captured my attention, and I saw two sheep coming out from under the roots of one of the trees. I went in closer to inspect and to my delight discovered that there was a cave under the tree roots. I stayed there with the sheep for an hour or so and then turned back.

When I rehearsed my adventures for my parents that evening, I heard the quick intake of breath and saw the blanched pallor of their faces. I did not understand their strong reaction.

My father stammered and said that he forbade me to ever go there again. Those were fairy rocks and were dangerous.

I laughed and said, "Father, you told me that you never believed in fairies. What could possibly be wrong with a cave in a hillside"?

Again, he forbade me to go there and would not talk about it again. Later I learned from Paddy that there were abandoned tin mines all over Glentogher that were used by smugglers to hide items from revenue agents and other officials. He told me that it was not safe to be found alone in those hills and that I should take my usual walk down to Trawbreaga when I wanted to wander.

I loved wandering down the lanes and across the fields, especially on a nice summer's day when the fuchsias were all in bloom. The bright red flowers covered the bushes that topped the ditches along the roads. The flash of colour was beautiful and cheery. In late summer, the heather began blooming purple on the hills and the prospect would become a full tapestry of colours. The greens and reds of the fields and ditches were set against the browns and purples of the heathery bog in the background. There would be splashes of other flowers blooming as well, yellows and oranges. Sometimes people would try to cultivate these flowers, but the plants never seemed to thrive in the garden like they did in the hills. I believe that God is a better gardener than the rest of us.

Most people would have planed herbs in their kitchen gardens. Thyme and cleavers were common. Mammy had been taught by her Mammy to know which plants or herbs would heal sickness. I heard her say that if a plant resembled a part of the body, then it must cure it. It seemed that no matter what the ailment, there would always be a plant, a flower, a root, or a leaf to be found. Mammy would describe what it looked like and where we could find it growing and explain exactly how to properly harvest it. Then we would run off to collect whatever she needed, even it if was way up in the hills or down in the woods.

Healing herbs were dried and hung from the ceiling. Berries, flowers and leaves were dried, labeled and stored for later use. Mammy had her remedies and elixirs too. Combinations of powdered roots, herbs and plants known for their healing properties lined the shelves of her kitchen dresser.

Heather blooming in the hills

After she was gone, I was so grateful that she had carefully tried to pass her great knowledge on to me. She taught me that buttermilk improved the complexion and if it was particularly bad, to use egg whites. Egg yolk was used to condition the hair and the water that potatoes had been boiled in could remove stubborn dirt from skin.

Once when Daddy was suffering from chilblains, the sore little red bumps on the tops of toes and feet, Mammy told him to head on up to the bog. I asked her what he was going to do up there.

She said, "He needs to take them feet up and place them into a bog hole. It will be very cold, but will cure the chilblains right enough. Otherwise he will be suffering for two weeks. With his whingin' and whinin' we will be suffering too."

Daddy limped on up the brae and came back a few hours later whistling. It was a startling change.

The work of making a living was spread out among the family. Even the smallest wean was given a chore to do. All the chores were vital to our survival. The work was hard, sometimes even back breaking, but we still took time to notice the good things, like a hawk making lazy circles in the sky, spying the rabbits or field mice below.

Sometimes I would just stop walking in the garden and, leaning up against the wall, I listened to see what I had been missing in my race through the day. My father used to say that if one stopped and noticed nature, ye might learn something and even be forewarned of changes coming in the weather.

Sometimes on a warmish summers' day in Ballyloskey, the sky would be so hazy that the white of the clouds seemed to come down and mingle with the fog rising from the earth. This would block all the views of the hills and down to Trawbreaga. There was no horizon. We would be in the middle of a white world surrounding our small farm. Even the sounds were muted in the white haze.

Some of the livestock would stand and some would just lay on the ground as if waiting for the clouds and fog to disperse. Local farmers will tell you that if the cattle were down upon the ground, it is going to rain, and if they are standing in the field, the weather will be fine. On those hazy white summer days it seemed that even the cattle were confused about what was going on with the weather.

In the winter the weather could be so bad for months on end. The sky was usually grey and the colour of it would blend into the grey of the water of Trawbreaga Bay. The only contrast

48

was the stark green of the trees against the whitewashed walls of the cottages. Even the blackthorn, whitethorn, whin bushes and the fuchsias in the ditches separating the fields were merely stark brown sticks. Most people painted their doors and window sills with either red or green to bring a bit of colour to the landscape.

Throughout the winter, we would all stay indoors, snug around the fire for warmth. On particularly nasty days when the wind was howling through the cottage, we would leave our beds only to use the necessary. Mammy would be up to tend the fire and cook the meals, and then she too would return to her bed, wrapping the bedclothes around her to recover her warmth.

It seemed that every few winters devastating illness would sweep through our community. Some said that it was the bad air from the bog settling in the cottage. If that was true, then illness should have hit every home equally, and it did not. Others decided that the water of some farms was not as pure as others.

We were told by Mammy to only drink water from the wells that she and my father said were for us. She said that the well down below the byre had a bad smell and we were not to drink from it. Influenza, the grippe or distemper would hit most homes every winter. Some years were worse than others. In our cold and damp climate, consumption was always a danger, especially to the very young or the very old.

Our house had its share of illness most winters, but we always looked forward to cleaning out our cottage coming up to Easter. It seemed that the sicknesses were thrown out with all the muck from the house each spring.

Each spring, Mammy would give us a tonic to cleanse us as well. Her favourite plants were ground ivy and elderberry. It seemed that most of the time when someone came calling for a remedy because they were ailing, Mammy would get them to agree to eat dried elderberries and make a tea of the ivy leaves. Dandelion leaves were also known as a cleansing tonic. Local plants, used wisely, cured illnesses and improved lives.

Chapter 8

Making Clothing

ammy's sewing and knitting needles were kept in a special box on the highest shelf above the hearth. She called it her workbox. In addition to needles, she had a cotton reel, a pair of heron scissors that looked like the bird, a sock darner, a thimble, a stitch picker and sewing pins.

I was allowed to look at them from time to time, but since Mammy said that they were hard to come by, we were not allowed to touch them. It was a solemn occasion, one that I took very seriously, when she presented me with my own knitting needles at age seven. I was old enough to begin learning to make the clothes, although I never thought I would be as good as she was at handwork. It was a point of pride to me that my needles were kept in the box next to hers.

There was always work to be done. In winter, daylight would be only six or so hours from sun up to sun down. When I was young, the homemade candles were precious and only used when necessary. The long winter's nights were spent working by the light of the fire.

The preparation of wool was tedious and time consuming. First Mammy would clean and sharpen her pair of shears, the

51

ones she got from her mother. The next day we would go out into the field to catch a ewe or two. Once caught, she grabbed hold of the horn, bending the head over a bit, began clipping the fleece away from the sheep. Mammy was great, she could clip the fleece so that it came off in one big lump. The fleece was dirty and ragged on the outside, but clean and fluffy on the inside.

Sometimes the ewes would throw off their fleeces in the springtime without shearing. Our job was to collect up the fleeces and carry them over to the wash tub that was kept just outside the house. Mammy laid the fleece out on a low stone wall and picked through the fibres. Fleeces are not uniform and she taught me which were the best parts for spinning.

The fleece was then carefully washed in a solution of urine diluted with water, and laid out on the stone wall to dry.

Woman Spinning on a Donegal Wheel

Beginning in the spring, Mammy would daily remind the boys to use the bucket at the bottom of the garden, so that she could

52

collect enough urine to wash and dye the wool. She also insisted that I had to be gentle with the washing or the wool would tangle or become felted.

Briars and pieces of sticks were removed and the fleece was oiled with paraffin oil, in preparation for carding. The clean, dry wool was brought into the house and Mammy would sit in the evenings, by the fire, carding the wool. She had two carding brushes. These were leather brushes with fine curved wire teeth and wooden handles that she used to comb the wool. Carding removes tangles and causes the fibres to lie side by side, ready for spinning. She would place the carded wool in her basket and when the day was bright enough, she would carry her spinning wheel outside.

The spinning wheels in Donegal are smaller than those made in other parts of Ireland. Mammy could use her wheel to spin wool either for knitting or making cloth as well as flax for linen shirts and shifts.

Flax would be harvested by pulling it from the ground after the flowers have dropped but before the seed heads were fully formed. We would tie it into sheaves and then let it dry. Mammy would then put the sheaves into the wash tub and steep them to "ret" or rot the woody fibres. We call this retting the flax. After a couple of days the flax was spread out to dry. It was important to separate the tow, the outer woody tissues from the bast. The brittle woody covering would be broken by beating it with a mallet to separate it from the long silky fibres. Next would come the scutching or cloving to remove the tow.

We were taught to be careful with making linen. Some other spinners did not take the time to do the hackling or combing of the flax fibres. This step divided the fibres into finer filaments ready for spinning. Mammy explained that proper hackling made the difference between rough looking and smooth linen thread. After spinning the thread into hanks or skeins, Mammy then boiled them in homemade potash and spread them in a tub to bleach.

This gave the linen its characteristic whiteness. The flax was then rolled into clews, or balls and was woven into linen cloth.

In winter, in addition to sewing shirts and working the wool for various pieces of clothing, we would also be busy repairing clothing, patching elbows and knees, re-sewing seams and darning socks by the light of the turf fire. Summer time was different; the days were so long that you could be up at four in the morning and work until almost midnight before it became too dark to see.

Many a summer's evening was spent with the local women of the neighbourhood, gathered in our house for an evening of carding, spinning, storytelling and singing. When the work was finished the men joined in for the ceili.

My father said that fairies were skillful spinners and that a prudent wife would, before retiring to bed, remove and hide the wheel band, so that the fairies could not work it. Mammy taught us that the wheel should never be taken out of the house after midnight lest we would be led astray by the people of the "other world."

Just after my Paddy died, the Tilley lamp came into fashion. The story was that these lamps had been invented in England by a John Tilley in the early 19th century. The lamps did not become readily used until after the Great War when the oil to light them was easier to obtain.

Everyone called the lamps Tilley or paraffin lamps because they were fueled by the oil we commonly called

Tilley Lamp

54

paraffin oil. These lamps gave off such a great light, with very little smoke or smell, that everyone bought one.

We would buy the paraffin oil by the gallon from the shop in town. When we ran low, I took my one gallon tin down to the shop and they filled it up from a big drum. The lamp did give off a great light, but I still preferred doing my handwork either outside or next to the open window. My girls out in Oregon said that this type of lamp was called a Coleman lamp and they called the oil kerosene.

Chapter 9

Thatching

hen I was a girl, most cottages had thatched roofs. Recently some farmers are turning to slate roofs, although they are not as lovely as a snug thatched roof. Thatching helps to make the home warm in the winter and cool in the summer.

Our local thatcher, Sean McLaughlin, was a real craftsman. It seemed that he was a far out relation of Paddy's sister-in-law, Nancy McLaughlin. No two thatchers worked exactly the same way. You could often look at a house and tell who had thatched it. Sean had learned the secrets of his success from his father and grandfather. He taught the trade to his sons and grandsons. The craft of the thatcher was one which many men could do, but few could do well. It often took many years of trial and error to gain the skill of proper thatching. Sean "Thatcher," as he was known, was his own master, tough, hardy and independent.

Many men would repair their own roofs, but when the roof needed a new application, they would call in the local craftsman for his considerable knowledge and experience. Our roof consisted of wooden couples held together by wooden pins. These couples were made from bog oak logs that the men found when they were cutting turf. There was something about being submerged in the bog for years that hardened the wood and made it sturdier than ordinary wood.

On our roof, runners ran at right angles to the couples from gable to gable at three foot spacings. Thin slats about four inches wide ran at right angles atop the runners, and spaced closely together, they supported the sod that the thatch rested upon. The thatch was put on in layers. The thatcher would move up the roof with a width of about two feet of flax, called a stroke. He would tie down the stroke with hemp rope that stretched from gable to gable every six inches. Other ropes were tied from front to back about the same distance apart. These ropes were tied to pegs of wood driven into the top edge of the walls.

Thatchers did not carry many tools. I seem to mind Sean "Thatcher" having a knife, a small mallet, a handmade rake and a thatching needle with which he secured the thatch to the roof. Sean "Thatcher" took great pride in his work, and the story is told locally how he would berate a farmer that was not taking proper care to repair his roof between thatching.

A good roof would last upwards of 15 years if proper care was taken. Thatch is a light weight material and is highly flammable, although rarely did it catch fire. Even if the occasional spark lodged in the thatch, it would not catch fire immediately, but would smoulder quietly for days. Every household would have a fire-hook ready by the hearth to avert a fire by removing the smouldering thatch.

Chapter 10

Harvest
1859

Due to the need of drying the hay and corn in the fields before the crops are carried home, harvest time continues from late summer clear to the edge of winter. The first hay cutting is usually mid-July, followed by flax, which is pulled from late July to mid-August. Wheat and barley are then harvested before the corn harvest in late September. Then there is potato-lifting in October. In bad years the hay might remain uncut until late August, with the late-cut corn still in the fields up to Christmas. Typically, however, all the harvest work was completed by All-Hallows.

The grass is commonly cut by a scythe or a sickle, and is shaken out by hand and spread thinly over the field. My father taught me when I was quite young, that the grass must be laid down carefully with the prevailing wind so that it is dried properly and easily turned.

Daddy loved it when he had a few good dry days during haying time. We could hear him whistling out in the field as he was turning the hay in the sun. He would be working away, the long sleeves of his white linen shirt rolled up past his elbows, sweat pouring off his face, as happy as he could be. Seeing the men out turning the hay in the summer time still brings a smile to my face and I remember my Daddy.

The cut hay must be thoroughly dried before it is placed on the slipe to be hauled by the pony and moved to the hay stack. When completed, the tall rounded stacks would be thatched with rushes and tied down with ropes to protect the hay from the weather and the wind. Some men used a long-handled scythe, but my father loved his sickle. He told me the story that his daddy, my Granda, always kept a beetle in a wee box, fastened to the end of the handle of his sickle. It was for good luck and gave the blade greater cutting power. His sickle was the one thing Daddy never wanted to share. When someone had to borrow it, it could never be passed directly from hand to hand. That would bring about bad luck. Instead, the sickle was thrown on the ground in front of the one who was going to borrow it and then the borrower picked it up.

Harvesting of the flax is still my least favourite season. It must be harvested after the small blue flowers have fallen off but before the seeds ripen. In our area, we call it lint. It is very hard work to process flax. Teams of farmers would work together on the flax harvest. First the reeds are pulled from the ground by hand. It is hard on the hands and back-breaking to stoop over pulling them out. Flax harvest is very labour intensive and requires many hands to complete each step. The beets or sheaves are then retted or steeped in a flax dam where soft peaty water had been standing for a few days to warm up. The retting usually takes about ten days until the lint is rotting. When it is sufficiently retted a foul smell permeates the farm. Then the slimy and ill smelling lint beets are removed from the dam and spread out on a field to dry out. Out on the field the reeds are not allowed to touch and dry into each other. When dry and brittle, the lint is gathered and tied into sheaves. This is the part that the children were expected to help with.

After it is dried, ideally it is ready for breaking and scotching, the beating which tenderized the tough stalks. The best lint was saved for weaving and hung in the rafters until needed. The rest was used for thatching. The best part of the lint harvest was the big night. Since it took upwards of thirty people to handle the lint, there usually was a big crowd of men for the work and the women to feed them, so at the end of the day there was a party. Music always seemed to follow after the hard work of the harvest.

The grain and corn harvest followed the lint harvest. Great care was taken in the fields to assure that no grain was lost from the ripe crops. Daddy often said that it was important to cut "low and clean – to the living earth" when cutting the crops. Once dried and bound into sheaves, the grain was brought into the barn for flailing. My father would spread a sheet onto the barn floor and open out a couple of sheaves at a time for beating. As the flailing got underway a steady rhythm developed and he believed that it was that rhythm that kept him going later on when he was feeling tired.

When our Paddy was about twelve, my father helped him make a flail. It was a blackthorn stick formed and used to thrash the corn after it was harvested. Blackthorn is used as hedging and the flowers are usually the first blooming in early March. The sticks are best cut in winter, when the sap is down. Paddy later explained to me how my father showed him to cut the stick with a knuckle near the crown that fit snugly into his hand. He then removed the spikes and small shoots without disturbing the bark. The stick was then lashed to a straight, stout, piece of timber and left near the fire for a few days. The warming of the stick helped to straighten it. After being warmed, the stick was left in the turf shed until spring. The cool dry air properly seasoned the stick. Our Paddy used that stick until he left for America. I mind that Hughie used it for years afterwards before he decided he needed to make another one.

Chapter 11

Musical Instruments

usic is a big part of our lives in the country. It is a comfort in the middle of the hardship. Most people around here can sing and they learn the songs from the time they are small. On the winter evenings, adults and young people will sing for one another or tell stories around the turf fire. On summer evenings, the ceili would be outside, commonly at the crossroads, with singing as well as a bit of dancing. Musical instruments were scarce, but those who had a fiddle, a tin whistle, or bodhran (a goatskin frame drum) were always welcome. When the visitors came, the children of the house would gather around waiting for the music to begin.

There were stories and gossip, sometimes for hours, and then by some invisible signal, the man of the house would stand up, tap his pipe out on the hearth and reach up onto the highest shelf away from the fire and carefully bring down the musical instrument. If it was a fiddle or bodhran, it would be tuned for a few moments, or the tin whistle would be blown out to prepare it for playing.

This ritual was solemnly witnessed by the children and accompanied by their collective intake of breath as they awaited the evening's entertainment. It was an exciting day when a wean was considered old enough by father or mammy to have gently placed into their small hands this instrument of great worth. It was the day that they began to make music guided by more experienced hands.

The knowledge of how to play the songs and the tunes was passed down from parent to child along with other life skills. Entertaining one's self and family was as important as other skills for there had to be joy in life.

Everyone was expected to learn their party piece. One or two songs or recitations would be memorized in anticipation of the big nights. The man of the house would call on each one in turn to do their party piece. Calls for more were always heard, whenever one had finished their first song. Although we all knew what songs or poems each one would do, the effort was always warmly welcomed and appreciated.

Bodhran drum

Tin whistles

Chapter 12

The Decision
14 April 1869

From my girlhood, I had dreamed of Big Paddy Newman asking me to be his wife. Sometimes as we strolled down the road, I picked flowers or watched the birds. He talked about his life in the future, his family, his home and his work. I got excited inside and thought,

"Now is the time, he is finally ready, now he is going to ask me."

But he never did.

After waiting all that time for Paddy to act, in the autumn of 1868 I decided that there was no hope of a proposal so I accepted Uncle Hughie and Auntie Mary's invitation to come to Boston. All of my friends from school were either married with a couple of weans or had already left. We heard their reports through the letters sent home to their parents.

Uncle Hughie had gone to America before I was born so I never knew him, but my eldest brother Paddy had gone out to them, when I was fifteen. That was also the year Maggie was born. He was only out there a month when he died tragically. The horse he was riding bolted; he was thrown and broke his leg badly. They tried to set the leg, but it became septic. We were told in the letter that he died peacefully, but I think that was Uncle Hughie's way of easing Mammy's burden. Everyone knows that the pain of such a wound is dreadful especially when it leads to blood poisoning.

My ticket finally arrived in the post just after Christmas. Mammy never talked about it, yet I knew that she did not want me to go. Even with knowing that, I could not stay here in Ballyloskey. Seeing Big Paddy Newman every day when he called in to collect my brother Hugh on their way to work in the fields was a torture. The two of them were now inseparable. Best mates, they said.

The morning after our Paddy had left for Boston, Big Paddy called at the house as usual, and without words Hugh collected his jumper and cap and stepped out into the morning air alongside Paddy, heading for the fields. He seemed to move into the place that had been our Paddy's as if it had been his own for years. I never asked Big Paddy if he thought about our Paddy. We never talked about the ones who were gone. And yet the ache in our hearts was ever present.

I had tried to ask Hugh in a roundabout way if Paddy was interested in anyone, if he was looking to settle.

Hugh would always just look at me with disdain and say to me, "Do not be silly, who would have a man with no land."

I wanted to shout out, "I would, I would have that man."

Instead, I just nodded at him, as if I understood. But I did not understand. I believed that we could make a good home together. We both knew and understood one another. We both worked hard and laughed together. What more did anyone need?

Paddy's father Philip worked three fields that he paid the leases on, surely he would be willing to share one with Paddy. Anyway there were always the land leases that were abandoned when folks left for America. I knew that there could be a way found to find land to work to support a family.

But after the years had passed by, I finally was forced to realise that no proposal was forthcoming. Day to day, month to month, nothing changed, so I decided to leave for America. In her letter home the previous summer, Auntie Mary had written of jobs available just for the taking. She worked in a big house, with a load of other Irish girls, cleaning and chatting. She said that it was great craic, especially when there was a party on. It was amazing how the rich folks lived.

The day I told Paddy that I had decided to go to Boston, he did not say anything. He just looked at me, expressionless. I turned and ran home, threw open the door and fell weeping into Mammy's arms. I really had thought that he loved me.

I began to talk more about my leaving and Paddy seemed even more remote. The more that he did not talk, the more I brought it up as a topic of conversation. Maybe it was just to irritate him. I do not know, but it seemed that we were compelled to dance this strange patterned dance, advancing and retreating without ever talking.

There was much to do to get ready. A trunk to carry my things magically appeared in the cottage one morning. I asked Mammy and my Daddy about it, but the only comment made was that the fairies must have brought it in. It was lovely, brass on the corners with leather straps that secured it tight.

Later I learned that it was the same trunk that Mammy's sister Margaret had brought back from America when she returned home years before. Granda thought that I should have it. I carefully packed a couple of dresses in the bottom of the trunk. My small clothes were added next. Then I put in an extra pair of shoes made for me by my father and a wee stove to boil the tay during the journey.

Since passengers had to have their own food with them, Mammy prepared the oaten scones for me. First she baked the scones as usual but the next day after they had set over night she ironed them with the heated clothes iron to harden them. Using the clothes iron that was heated in the fire would dry the moisture out of the scones so they would be preserved and last for the entire journey. These ironed scones were tough going on the teeth sometimes, but you could soften them a bit by dunking them in tay or by putting your mouth on them for a while before actually biting into them. The scones were wrapped in flour sacking and placed in the trunk.

To finish packing, I put in my sewing kit, two blankets that I had stitched, and the lace table cloth that I had made. My trousseau was going to America. A family from Glentogher was journeying on the same ship, and they offered to take my trunk to Derry along with their things. That offer made Mammy feel relieved. The woman also said that she would look out for me. She knew my Uncle Hughie and would see that I was safely delivered to him in Boston.

The morning finally arrived, Tuesday the 13th of April, my last day in Ballyloskey. My trunk had gone ahead the day before to Derry and on the morrow I would need to board the ship. People kept arriving all morning just to say cheerio and God speed. A plan for a party was organised. Later that night we would all meet up at Loch Inn in the bog and walk down to the ship in the morning. There would be dancing and all sorts of carry on. Someone's leaving could be great craic, always an excuse for a party. Except for me, this time was different. It was to be me leaving. I had such mixed feelings. After the morning chores I told Mammy that I would be back after a bit. First I walked around our small farm and said goodbye to the chickens and the cow. Then I went down to the small stream at the bottom of the field and sat on a rock to bathe my feet. I thought of all the work, the chores, the various efforts and even the life that I had lived here. I dried off my feet on the hem of my skirt and then I wandered up the road, past McLaughlin's and up past the Newman's.

My eyes firmly looked straight up the road, I could not look into the street that for so many years I had hoped would be my home. I had envisioned me opening the door in the mornings to let in the fresh air, baking the scones on the fire and setting them in the window to cool, churning the butter in the afternoon looking out over Trawbreaga Bay and sweeping the floor in the evening after the day's finish. Those dreams had vanished and although I wiped away a tear, with resolve I squared my shoulders and walked up into the bog. At the top of the hill, I approached the lone tree in the hills where I had often escaped. It was a place of peace where birds would gather in the summer and sing to me of places they had seen. It was also a place of solemn contemplation during the cold winter months and I had spent many an hour there sorting out my thoughts and ideas growing into the woman that I was. I felt the need to say goodbye.

I had not realised that I was almost running up Ballyloskey, as if to escape. I slowed my pace and began to mentally note every sound and image. I believed that I would need to have these memories stored away for the times over the years when my heart would long for home. After an hour's time, I returned home, renewed and even firmer in my resolve to leave. I had made the right decision. My life was to begin across the sea and with my face firmly turned toward America, I entered the cottage for my final goodbyes.

It was a big production to leave Ballyloskey and head for Derry. You could make the trek walking in about five hours. A horse and cart would make it in half the time. As a teenager I had walked the distance before. We had known when the tall ships would be at Derry Quay and when the planned sailing was, so we would head over the hills for Quigley's point or Moville. We would watch the small currachs, the Irish skin boats used by local fishermen, taking passengers out to the ship and then stand along the shore waving to the ones as they sailed away. We would often remark that we were the last vision of Ireland to the ones leaving for America.

There is a local story from around the time I was born that a ship was anchored off the Quay in Moville. It was full. All of the passengers' baggage and precious things had been loaded during the day and everyone was waiting for the tide in the morning. The passengers, Captain and the crew were all in Moville celebrating their last night. Then a hue and cry was heard that changed to keening as each one looked out toward the horizon and saw the ship in flames. Something had caught fire aboard and everything was ablaze. The ship burned to the waterline and then sunk just out from the pier. There had been no one aboard to put out the fire.

No one was harmed, but the belongings of all the passengers were lost. Their hopes and dreams of a better life in America were dashed that night and they had to walk back to their homes and families and begin once more to rebuild their fortunes in order to try again later.

For some of those people, the experience destroyed them. Others looked forward with hope and determination as they again gathered to themselves the provisions needed to make the crossing of the ocean. They would attempt to save what they could, but most people made the crossing on money sent home from America by those who had gone before.

After that, people were careful. They would not have their things put on board until it was time to leave, even though the shipping companies wanted the trunks a day ahead, they were not loaded onboard until the morning of departure.

My life sure changed that day. Part of me was so happy and another part of me was so angry. That morning I awoke with the knowledge that it was to be my last day in Ballyloskey, and by the next evening I was back in my parents' home, in my own bed. But I get ahead of myself.

As the day unfolded, I was able to say goodbye to all who were dear to me, except for Paddy. He seemed to be staying away. Apparently, no one else but me noticed.

Finally the time came for all of us young ones who were leaving to walk up to Loch Inn, the wee lake in the bog and meet up for the party. With all the friends and relations along for the send-off, we made a massive group. The excitement was tangible.

Out came the food and drink, the blankets to sit upon as well as musical instruments for entertainment. The sky was clear with just a hint of a moon. It was a beautiful night. There was laughter, plenty of drink, songs, recitations and even dancing. Great craic. It was a wonderful party. We carried on until sometime in the night, one by one, we all fell asleep making our beds under the stars.   Paddy was there, of course, and we did dance together, but we really did not talk much. He seemed so distant, even angry, and I did not want to know what it was. For years he had had his chance to speak, and had not. Now I did not want to hear from him.

A few hours before the dawn we awoke, gathered our things and began the rest of the walk from the bog, then along the Foyle to Derry City. By then we were a huge caravan of people, and more seemed to join us as we journeyed. Everyone was walking and laughing in the first lights of morning, the dew wetting our shoes and clothes as we made our way.

The sun rose ahead of us, first peering at us over the mountains beyond Derry City at about half six. The anticipation seemed to move us along a little quicker and it felt great to be a part of it. We arrived at the Quay about a half an hour later, and found the ship preparing to sail for nine. We had about an hour's wait before we could climb aboard. Everyone was in the departures area of the Quay, chatting and laughing, standing in their own little groups with those they knew.

Only Paddy stood apart from the rest. He looked so alone. Yet every time I glanced his way, he just stared at me with his head turned slightly to the side, just watching. It was odd. There were nine of us from the Carn area who were heading out. We had known each other from school days and were excited to begin this next adventure together. My parents had not come along to the Quay; there was work to do they said. I think that it would have been too emotional at the Quay, so we had said our goodbyes the previous evening at the cottage door before I left.

The ship, the *Minnehaha*, known as "The Green Yacht from Derry," was the most famous clipper owned by the McCorkell Line. She was headed for Boston. She had been making the crossing since being built in Canada in 1860. She was a beautiful sailing ship, able to cross the Atlantic in all weather including the winter.

Some of her passengers were going on to Philadelphia to relations there. During the waiting time, I checked with the steward to be sure that my passage had been paid and that my trunk had been loaded. Everything was in order and I was heading to America. I cannot explain the feelings that were in my heart and the thoughts that were in my head at that moment. The whistle blew for the passengers to load and I stepped forward to hand in my ticket.

No one else seemed anxious to board, so I was alone on

The *Minnehaha*

the gangplank. I walked a couple of steps up the incline and looked over the Foyle toward the hills of Donegal. I was lost in the memories flooding my mind, of home and hearth, of heather and bog, of family and times gone by. The hustle and bustle of the Quay faded away as I wistfully looked towards home.

I think that a tear rolled down my cheek and then I shook meself and took a deep breath and let the excitement of the coming adventure crowd out those melancholy thoughts. I was heading out to start my life. For years, I had waited at home, hoping to start a different life in Ballyloskey. That life had been denied me, so I was going to find my new life in America.

As I stood there, with my hand grasping the rail, not yet on the ship and not still on the shore, I heard a voice calling my name. I looked for the source and realised that it was that big eegit of a man standing on the pier, the one that had not talked to me for weeks.

Paddy then noticed that he had caught my attention.

He stepped forward, took off his hat and began to turn it over and over, crushing it between his two massive hands.

He said, "Well, Mary...Mary, will ye come down off the gangplank, walk back to Ballyloskey and marry me? Ye just canna go."

I was stunned. What could I say? My future looked to be in Boston. He already had plenty of opportunity over these past five or six years to ask me to be his wife if that was what he wanted. I had made my intentions and desires obvious to him and he had seemingly ignored them.

Here he was at the very last minute, asking me the question that I had dreamed of. In the very moment that I was leaving to begin my life, he was asking if I would change all that and return home and marry him.

I stood there for I do not know how long, just looking down at him, slowly shaking my head.

He tilted his head a little and raised one eyebrow, shrugged his shoulders as if to say, "What? Well, I am asking ye now."

So I laughed, looked at my would-be travelling companions and said, "Well, ye go on then, I am for Ballyloskey."

I ran down the gangplank, the ones behind me parting as a giant wave. Some laughed, others cried, some shook their heads, but I did not hear what they had to say. I was just looking at the one face that was looking back at me. I stood in front of him.

He said, "So, that is that."

And I said, "Yes, that is that."

He then tried to get my trunk unloaded from the ship, but it was too late. It was in the cargo hold and impossible to remove, there was not time before the ship was set to sail. So my trousseau, containing all my precious things, was going to America and I was staying.

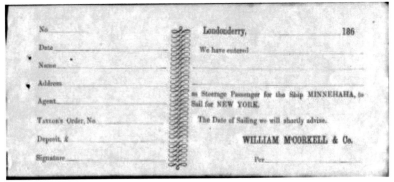

A Passenger Ticket from William McCorkell & Co.

I had a moment's twinge of worry when I thought of the great care that had been taken to prepare and pack my things. My parents had sacrificed so that I could have the necessities for the travel. When I told the ship's purser I was not going, he gave me the ticket back so that I or someone else could use the passage at a later time.

At least Uncle Hughie's money would not be wasted. I canna mind who actually used the ticket in the end, but I do remember having a concern about the effort that my parents had made to ready me for the trip. I knew that they would be delighted to see me back again, but losing all my earthly possessions that were heading to America was a cost that would not easily be recovered. Times were so hard and money so scarce.

We began the long walk back home with the others who had travelled to Derry to say goodbye. At the time, I was so happy that my feet were barely touching the ground. I realised that I really was going to start my new life, just where I had always wanted to be, in Ballyloskey with that big eegit.

But I never did ask him why it took him so long to propose. Maybe he was not sure that I would say yes. Maybe he wanted more for me in life than the hard existence that we had before us in Ballyloskey. He knew that hard life very well and also knew that there was great opportunity in America. Maybe he wanted to be willing to let me go to that great opportunity, but at the last minute, he could not. I could tell as we walked back home from Derry City that he was glad to have me by his side. There was never any big outpouring of emotion or affection. That just was not Paddy. We walked in silence.

The next day Paddy called at my parents' cottage as usual to collect Hugh to go to the fields.

As he was going out the door, he turned back to me and said, "I have already met with the Priest to arrange for the banns to be read. With no objections from anyone, we will be wed in six weeks' time."

Of course no one had any objections to our wedding. All our relations and connections knew that we were for each other. There had never been anyone but Paddy for me and it seems that there was never anyone but me for Paddy. It did take him a long time however to get the courage up to ask the question. He almost lost me.

Chapter 13

Our Wedding
Saturday, 15 May 1869

Paddy and I began our lives together on our wedding day. Since my trunk with my best clothes had remained on the ship, Mammy and I had quickly sewed a new trousseau for me over those six weeks. There had been so much to do that the days had flown by.

I awoke that morning to hear my Daddy say in the quiet of the dawn, "Well, Kate, today is the day, the day our wee girl never thought would come. Today she will leave our home and become his wife."

Mammy said, "Ach, John, how am I to stand it? I will miss her so."

He laughed and said, "Kate, Kate, she will just be up the hill and across the road, three fields away. You can still see her each day. She will be in our house, you will be in her house. It will be grand."

I heard her whisper amidst the sobs, "I know, John, but my wee girl is going to be another man's wife, a woman with her own house, starting today. It will never be the same."

In stillness I lay, not wanting to disturb my last moments of being a daughter and a child of the house.

I did not know what that new life would bring, but like any young woman, I was full of hopes and dreams. I knew that we would have a wonderful family of well-behaved weans who were strong like their father and beautiful like their mother. At least that is what I told Paddy. I knew also that there would be hard times. Everyone had hard times, but I had my wee house, and my mother-in-law, Nancy, was very kind. She loved me. She told me that I was the making of her boy. She had almost lost hope herself that he would settle. I knew that we would live well with one another.

That is not always the case when the new bride is moved into the house on the wedding day and the old woman is pushed from her hearth to make room for the new woman of the house. For those women, both the young and the old, the first days of resentment and discouragement set the tone for the rest of their lives. Not so with Nancy and me. I had been in and out of her house since I could walk up the road following Paddy and Hugh. She had been the first one to teach me how to properly churn the butter and how to make a scone. Her scones always outshone mine, but she was never harsh with me as I kept on trying.

That morning, I helped Mammy with the chores as usual, and then I dressed quickly. We were to be at the chapel at 11 for the wedding mass. On the way down to the chapel, Nancy and Mammy spoke of their own wedding days. Philip and Nancy had been married in her home place. At that time it was tradition to have the sacraments in the house. The chapel in Carn had recently been completed and everyone was getting used to gathering there for Sunday mass, but all other events were overseen by the Priest in the house. By the time that Mammy married a few years later, that practice was changing.

At the synod at Thurles in 1850, Archbishop Paul Cullen decreed that the sacraments of baptism, marriage and confession were to be held in the chapel and not in the recipients' home. Locally, Priests began the arduous task of convincing their parishioners that the long-standing tradition should change. That is why, 19 years later on our wedding day, no one expected marriage masses to occur anywhere else but the chapel.

My big day was a blur. Mostly I was excited to see the day done but I do have a few memories: Leaving out the front door of my homeplace and walking toward my soon-to-be-husband Paddy; the pleased look on his face probably mirrored my own; standing together in the chapel in front of the Priest and our family and friends. I was suddenly nervous.

During the vows I looked straight ahead at his broad shoulders. I could not look up at his face. I did not know if I would laugh or cry. I did not want to embarrass meself or Paddy. I had looked forward to that day since I was small and then when I actually was becoming his wife, the seriousness of the vows and commitment to each other and our lives together fell upon me and I was overwhelmed.

The Priest said, "I pronounce you man and wife. You may kiss your bride."

Paddy lifted my chin with his fingertips and gingerly kissed me on the lips, in front of everyone. I blushed with embarrassment, yet suddenly felt better. The Priest then announced us. I was Mrs. Paddy Doherty. I laughed as we walked down the aisle and into the sunshine. Everyone came up to the house for the party.

I had a wonderful day. That night, Paddy and I were exhausted from the strain of so many things happening as well as the excitement of getting married. As is common to newlyweds, we hesitantly approached our marriage bed, but any awkwardness between us was worked out over time.

The day after our wedding dawned bright and clear. It was my first day to awaken in the cottage as the mistress of the house. So many things had changed from the day before. I woke early, the light streaming in through the window.

I said to meself, "Right ye are, Mary, ye should start as ye mean to go on."

Only thing was, I did not know exactly where to start.

Nancy had told me, when I first came up to the house, that I was welcome and to put my things wherever I thought they would be most useful. This was now my home and I was the woman of the house, so I should do whatever I felt should be done. But that first morning, I just stood there not knowing what to do. Quietly, she cleared off a shelf in the dresser for my dishes and set my churn next to hers. But when she put my stool closest to the fire, I knew then that she had really welcomed me.

Susannah, Big Shan's wife, called at the house with their six children. She instructed them all to welcome their new "Auntie Mary."

At first they looked around the cottage confused. Young Bernard said, "Where is our new Auntie Mary? I's only see Granny Nancy and wee Mary Hudie."

Susannah laughed, pushing them forward and said, "I told ye, your Uncle Paddy has married wee Mary Hudie and she is now your auntie. Now welcome her proper."

They filed past me, from Annie who was ten down to baby Paddy who was just past a year, each one shaking my hand, the girls making a small curtsey and the boys a wee bow. Susannah later confided to me that the weans had practised a great deal at their house, in hopes of making a good impression.

I had known Susannah all my life. She was from the house just at the corner of Upper and Lower Ballyloskey Road. Two fields over from my homeplace, we all called it Lower Town. Twelve years my senior, she married Big Shan Newman, Paddy's brother, in December 1857 and moved into the cottage across the road. Paddy's and Shan's bachelor uncle Cornelius Newman was ailing and he invited the newlyweds to share his house. Susannah cared for him until he died later the next year. Big Shan took over Cornelius' land lease and the cottage became their home.

Susannah had so much more experience in life than I had. She became a sister to me. I relied on her. I loved my own sisters Sarah and Maggie, but since they were only six and three when I married, their lives were on a different timeline than mine.

Paddy's mother Nancy and I made room for each other as we worked side by side to care for our family, especially our men. She told me that first day that she knew that I would be a good wife to him and a good mother to the weans that would come. I blushed when I thought of the marriage bed. On that day she began to call me daughter.

Nancy was a kind and amiable woman. Philip seemed stern and a little withdrawn. He had a highly intelligent look about his face and when he would speak, it was wise to listen, for his rare sayings contained deep and philosophical meanings. He obviously was a heavy thinker, and thought long and hard when he was alone in his quiet times. He was not given to laughter much, nor joviality, although Nancy was quick to laugh and find the humour in otherwise awkward or difficult situations. I certainly could see parts of each of them in my husband. Even through the drudgery of the daily tasks there was a contagious lightness in Nancy's speech. She made everyone feel welcome and her cookpot on the stove seemed to be bottomless because she could stretch it to feed anyone who stopped in. She would stand at the half door greeting those along the road, inviting any who were so inclined to pull up a stool to the hearth and have a wee cupa and a bit of soup. She always knew what was happening in both our little world of Ballyloskey as well as the greater world beyond. With her gentle ways and knowledge of local herbs she would often be called to help those who were ill, ailing or feeling poorly.

Even if someone just needed to have a bright spot in their day, she would take a pot of soup around and chat a bit to buoy the spirits. I often would go along with her and watch her as she helped others.

Even though she was not inclined to gossip, she seemed to know everything about everyone in the area.

If I happened to say something unkind or gossipy about someone, she would raise one eyebrow, tilt her head and softly say, "But sure, have not they had a hard time of it?"

Then she would recite a situation or story about the person and then my heart would be softened toward them so I would not repeat the unkind thing.

"Ach, the poor critter, they just need a bit of concern and they will be all right."

That was the way of her.

On the rare occasions when Philip had a drop of the cratur (the poitin that was brewed locally), he would go on and on about the great history of the O'Dochartaighs, the Lords of Inishowen. Nancy let him rave on, and then after a time, she would stop in the middle of whatever work she was doing, either the brushing the floor or stirring the cookpot or whatever.

Showing her regal stature and stance, she would say to him, "Yous O'Dochartaighs are just the newcomers around here, we McLaughlins were the Lords of Inishowen far earlier than yous O'Dochartaighs. We were here when yous were just down in the Lagan Valley chasing around after your small herds of cattle."

Laughing she would turn back to her labours.

Chapter 14

Expecting Our Baby
June 1870

y brother Hugh returned from Carn and came up to our cottage late one afternoon. He had heard from the grocer that a tall ship was seen off Malin Head and that she would be docked at the Derry Quay on the morrow. I took no notice of the news as my mind was focused on our coming wean. There was much to do in preparation for a child.

Mammy and I had saved the flour sacking to make the baby clothes and nappies. She taught me how to make all the necessary clothes and blankets for our baby. By washing and bleaching the sacking that flour came in, the cloth became very white and soft, the perfect fabric for our new wean. Mammy even cut up an old linen shirt of Paddy's. By quilting a threadbare wool blanket between two linen layers, she made a nice warm blanket to swaddle our baby.

Although I did not want the risk of an early birth, in those long summer days that year, I felt that I was ready. It is often said that one never knows how long a first baby will take to come, and I still had a couple of months remaining.

Mary's trunk that returned to Ireland from Boston

So I did not pay much attention when a wagon arrived at our door the next day. I was surprised when Paddy called me out to the street. Willie Diver had been in Derry the day before when the ship had docked and been unloaded. He was expecting a shipment from Boston. One of the dockmen heard him mention that he was from Carn and asked if he could take along a parcel for a Mary Doherty "Hudie" of Ballyloskey. The parcel turned out to be my well-travelled trunk. It had arrived in Boston and Uncle Hughie had sent it back to me.

Paddy hauled the trunk into the cottage. We laughed as we opened it and noticed that it still contained the oaten scones and crackers that I had put into it for the onward journey. They were stale and not much good to us, so we fed them to the chickens. Uncle Hughie and Aunt Mary had included a wedding present in the trunk.

It was a beautiful dinner set, eight plates and bowls plus a large platter. The set was beautiful; white with a blue border. I had never seen anything so exquisite in my life. I carefully washed them and put them on the dresser. It took me a while to use any of the dishes, I was so afraid of breaking them.

The Platter from Mary's dinner set

Since I was increasing, and the clothes from my trunk did not fit me anymore, Mammy and I decided to re-work them. I was able to cut up a shift to make clothes for the baby. Mammy had finished up tatting some lace for the collar and sleeves. The baby clothes were so beautiful. After her passing, I would finger the tatting sometimes when I especially missed Mammy and somehow was comforted. I used them as each of the weans were born and packed them carefully away when they became too small. Later I reworked the rest of the fabric from my dresses to make other dresses for my girls as they grew older.

That was just the way of it. We used what we had as we needed it and then reworked it to have a second or third use, until the cloth was all used up. When carefully cutting down a dress, the worn shiny parts could be cut out and used for rags. Then the remaining fabric would look brand new for a smaller girl's dress.

I could turn a skirt and move the seams and no one would know that it had been reworked. I was often pleased that I could turn a good seam. My girls would usually look better turned out than we had the means for. Some of the clothes they wore were presents sent from America, but most of the clothes were just reworked from someone else. Many local women could make a better scone or pot of butter than me, but I was always able to trade with them for their wares because of my handiness with a needle.

We had to rely upon one another so that the whole community could survive. Even though the Great Hunger had been over 20 years before, the fear of blight still hung over the local farmers. Each spring we would have the seeds blessed by the Priest and then pray mightily at mass for the plants and the coming harvest. We had to rely on what we grew or could trade with others to sustain ourselves. Our milk came from the cow in the byre and if she was ailing, that could cause us great worry. If the chickens ceased to lay, we lost a major portion of our daily protein food. Our neighbours would give us what they could spare when we had need just as we would give to them in their difficult times. We all looked after one another.

Although there was a doctor at the Fever Hospital connected to the Workhouse in Carn, no one ever called for him during a birth unless it had gone wrong. Mrs. Mary Ann McGuinness was the handy-woman who was called in to assist.

She had learned from her mother who had learned from her mother and on before. We always called on the McGuinness women to help bring the weans into this world. Mary Ann had a quiet and calm nature, and yet she could order the biggest man about if it was necessary and they would all obey.

Earlier that spring, in March, Susannah had given birth to a wee girl. Matilda they called her. She had come too early and only survived a few days. Although she was Shan and Susannah's seventh wean and fourth daughter, they felt the loss keenly and were a long time grieving. I realised that I too was increasing shortly after Matilda's passing. I was concerned about mentioning my joyful news so soon after their great sadness, but Paddy was over the moon, and said that he had to announce it to the entire world. We called in on Shan and Susannah to tell them the news.

A look passed between the two of them, and for a moment I was sure that we should not have told them yet. Then Susannah jumped up from her stool by the fire, hugging me tight, she insisted that I sit down next to her.

"When do you think that the wean will arrive?" she asked excitedly.

"What have you and your Mammy already prepared? I have a few things that I can let you use. They are well used, having been through six weans already."

I was so impressed by her strength and her friendship. We spent countless hours together through that spring and summer. Susannah willingly answered all my questions and mentioned other things that I was not even aware that I would need to know. She was a true friend.

I appreciated her sacrifice to be in attendance for my first birth, while still carrying her recent grief. Paddy's sister Mary Hirrell was delivered of Daniel, a bonnie wee boy, just a few days after my wedding anniversary in May. Having wee Daniel about was a joy and a healing for the entire family.

It was about four in the morning on the Saturday just before the August fair day when I awoke in terrible pain. In my life I had seen that birthin' a baby was terribly difficult on the woman, but at first I could not understand what was wrong with me. After a few waves of the pains coming and going, I decided that it was time to wake Paddy. He, like me, seemed surprised that the day had finally arrived, although I felt like I was as big as a house. A few hours passed and Mammy arrived in to check on me as was her custom. She sent Paddy across the fields for Mrs. McGuinness.

I felt a great comfort when she arrived and took charge. She had helped birth all the local babies for as long as I could remember. Although childbirth was dangerous, and I knew many a family who had lost both the mammy and the wean, I knew I was in good hands.

I canna mind all the details of my labour and wee Mary's birth. I know that it was almost time for the tea when she finally arrived. And I do remember the strong feeling of love swelling up within me as I looked into her wee bright blue eyes blinking, looking up into mine. I was laughing as Mary Ann was handing me what looked like a sheaf of parsley to chew on after the childbirth, Paddy quietly stepped in, stooping down with his hat in his hand to come in the doorway. He did not say a word, just looked at our new wean with awe. That was the way of him for every birth. I am not sure where he was waiting outside the cottage, but each time he seemed to know the exact moment when everything was cleaned up and the midwife all finished.

The next day was the fair day and although Paddy was meant to go to town, we both stayed back in the cottage just marveling at what we had done. We both were so chuffed, it was as if our wean was the most incredible baby ever to be born.

The next year and a half were a delight. Paddy and I watched in amazement as our beautiful baby girl first began to smile and then laugh. She was a bonnie wean with the sweetest disposition.

Paddy would rush in from the fields, heading straight for her cot, scooping her up and swinging her around the room, he would ask, "Well how is the wee missus today? What did ye do all day? You are such a good wee girl."

And she was.

We had hardly any bother from her; she was content to sit by my side as I worked through the day. When our Kate arrived eighteen months later, Mary was the biggest help to me. Although she was not yet two years of age, she would fetch the nappies or the bottle of milk, sometimes noticing that the wean needed something without me even having to ask. She was aware when the wee baby had a need and would try her best to manage. She was so precious to us.

Mammy died just after our Kate turned a year. I still feel the loss of her. She had been ailing for about a month. At first I was worried that it was the fever and that the weans would catch it. She reassured me that it was not the fever and that she was all right. I did notice that she was eating flax seed and dried whin berries with her meals, both of these are known to help with the treatment of sugar diabetes, but when I asked her about it, she denied being ill.

It was not until after she died, when my sister Sarah and I were washing her body, with the help of Mrs. McGuinness, before laying her out, that we noticed the tumors and ulcers on her breasts. She had died of cancer. I then remembered years before her telling me that flax seed and whin berries are well known in the treatment of cancer, especially breast cancer. I wept as I thought of her suffering without us knowing. There were many times in the coming years that I missed her wisdom, not only with cures and tinctures, but also concerning rearing weans and managing a household.

Chapter 15

Horses
1874

I have never been a great one for horses. I am of the mind that if it is bigger than you, you really ought to let it go on its way. But some men have such a love for these horses that they have to own them and work with them. They have a need to tame them. I would just as soon walk.

But I do remember the time that our Hugh tried to break a colt. The animal was beautiful, truth be told. He was probably about a year and a half or two at the time. The colt was a good height, the top of his head being the same as the top of our Hugh's shoulders. The colt had been in the lower field of Holymount, the Dr. Layard's hunting lodge, for the previous couple of months.

Every day our Hugh had the job to care for the animal. In addition to mucking out the stalls in the outbuildings, he was to feed it, talk to it, and gently calm it. Hugh worked at getting the colt to trust him. He would brush it all over and trim its hooves and tail. After a while, he began rubbing the colt with a bag of old rags, teaching it to stand still. Rather like a large dog, it would be standing at the corner of the field waiting on our Hugh. It would prance around a bit as he approached.

After a time, the day finally arrived that our Hugh decided it was time to put a saddle on the back of the horse. After the usual routine, he brought the saddle into the field and let the horse smell it. Then he touched the old saddle all over the horse, to get it used to it, as he had been doing with the rags over the weeks before.

I do not even know where the saddle came from, probably from The Landlord's son. Our Hugh was a big man of about 24 and knew his way around the horses. He had spent many long hours working with this animal. Our Hugh then laid the saddle on the colt's back with the cinch hanging down one side. He reached under and rubbed the animals belly as if to say, this will be fine, you will be all right. He eventually got the saddle cinched up properly and the colt began to fidget. The tail was flicking and the ears were laid back, with perceivable impatience.

I do not know why our Hugh did not notice these same behaviours, but he did not. I was about to call out to him, to warn him, but just at that moment, our Hugh decided, now was the time. He stepped one foot up into the stirrup, and threw his body over the back of the animal like he was a sack of grain with two legs hanging off one side of the colt. He looked so funny. I almost laughed. For some reason that horse bolted and there was our Hugh trying to hang on as hard as he could with the kicking and the bucking and the flailing.

Perhaps only ten or fifteen seconds lapsed, though it seemed longer. This large animal was out of control, running back and forth, back and forth, jumping with all fours off the ground in between. Head down, back up and then circling to the right and then to the left. All of a sudden it was over, and there was our Hugh lying on his back looking up at the sky with the colt standing about 15 feet away, shivering and foaming, breathing heavily, huffing and snorting, just looking at him.

It was a horrible experience. It was another three months of coaxing and training before our Hugh could get the saddle near that animal, and himself thinking that he knew how to break horses.

The Landlords' roads were off limits to the local folks. The Landlord had a right-of-way between fields and across farms. These paved and tree-lined roads were created to separate the upper class from the peasants. Those who travelled the roads whether in open or closed carriages would not need to see fields or hovels or anything about the lives of those less fortunate; the fine folk could just enjoy the pleasant trees. Our Paddy and Big Paddy would get onto the road down in the lower field near the washing stream and then walk along like they controlled the world until just past Canny's field. They would not stay on too long in case they would be caught, as they just wanted to prove to themselves that they were good enough to be on the road too.

I would be the lookout for them, to make a low whistle if someone came along. I was afraid that if they were caught, they would be punished. Punishment could take many forms, depending on who was exacting the penalty. They never were caught, but the fear was there all the same.

Holymount, the Landlord's hunting lodge, sat just at the bottom of our fields. It was originally built by a Doctor Henry Layard who moved to Malin from Tyrone and married a local girl. The family actually lived away, but would sometimes come to visit their home here. Even if no one was at home there very often, it loomed in our vision and in our minds.

There was always conversation centered round what the fine folk were doing, who was expected at the house, and what they were doing. Since the young ones worked there (the girls in the house as scullery maids and cleaning staff under the direction of the housekeeper, and the boys in the barns and on the grounds) we heard all the gossip about the relations and connections of the Youngs and the Harveys and others of those living in the Big Houses. But there was always the fear that one of those men of fashion would take notice of one of the local girls and be the ruin of her. Girls on their own could not easily avoid those kinds of advances, so the local girls were always instructed by their

93

mothers to work in groups of three together and to never look any of those fine folks in the eye.

Every once in a while we heard about a girl who had not followed that counsel from her family and was left with the consequences and the shame. A girl in that situation would be shunned by her family and neighbours and was usually sent away to Canada or America if the fare could be raised. If not, there were places down the country to which they would be sent.

There was a local girl who had such a baby in a convent in Dublin. The baby died, some say fortunately, and the girl was sent to a relation in Canada. It was a harsh end to a situation not entirely of her making. There never seemed to be any consequence to the men of fashion who pushed themselves on these innocent young girls. I wondered why they did not carry the same burden of shame. Everyone said that they were just different than regular folk.

In the autumn, the Landlord had his hunting parties. The local boys, including our Hugh and Big Paddy readied the stables and the horses. It was exciting for all except the fox. There were many guests and friends who arrived during the days prior to the hunt. Music and laughter would fill the evening breezes from Holymount. The boys would have to go over early on the hunt day. They saddled up all the horses and then prepared to be beaters for the actual hunt. The red-coated hunters would mount, the dogs barking and restless.

Typically the fog was swirling around, giving the fox a fighting chance. The horn would sound and they would be off. The boys would be at the end of the selected field beating the fences and ditches with sticks to flush out the game, whether bird or fox. I could never stand to watch the actual hunt. It did not seem fair to the poor animals. Hugh and Paddy would just laugh at me.

Commonly in the evenings, we would all enjoy sitting around the cottage sharing stories about the events of the day. It was the time most men and women spent together for during the day time our duties kept us apart. Most days Paddy would come in the house around lunchtime for his dinner if he was working nearby fields. Other days I would take a scone of bread and fill a bucket with tea and milk, before going out into the field to bring him some food. During those meal times there was not much conversation that passed between us.

Most of my conversations were with women. Topics included our thoughts and ideas concerning child rearing, food preparation, tending the sick, what the neighbours were doing, everything that went on in our townland. Even news of world events would trickle into our conversations. Since Mammy died, Susannah became a great help to me. It seemed that we were up and down the brae daily into each other's cottage. Even though she had the great grief of losing Matilda the same year that I had Mary, we seemed to share the joy of increasing with each other.

In 1872, she had Ellen a week after I was delivered of our Kate. Susannah had the twins John and William in March of 1874. Poor baby William was just too tiny to survive past a few days and it was while I was helping Susannah for those next few weeks, that I began to realise that I was increasing too. Our Philip was born that October. In May of 1876 she delivered Rose just two weeks before I had Anne. Her wee Rose only survived a few hours. Two years later I had our John, and about three weeks later she delivered Joseph. She had Susan 18 months after Joseph and our Paul was born six months after that, but in June of 1882 she delivered Benedict two weeks after our poor wee Bernard was born and died.

She had helped me by washing his wee body for burial, all the while the tears streaming down both our faces. Even though it had been a couple of days, I had not yet recovered from the birthin' and was lying exhausted in my bed. I was so grateful that we had been able to call in the Priest to have wee Bernard baptised before he died. My labour had been too long and he was too tiny, it was apparent early on that he would not survive. So Paddy left to collect the Priest Father Philip O'Doherty.

Susannah and I were a great comfort to each other in the trials of life, and we also enjoyed sharing the joyful times of rearing weans. The wee things that they said to us or the funny stories we shared as they tried to be all grown up. I was sure that my Mammy had laughed with her friends over the things that I had done, just the same as Susannah and I did over our own weans. We found joy in the small experiences of life and tried not to worry about the bigger problems.

I do mind that the harvest of 1879 was the worst in over 60 years. We were all worried about the lack of food. The autumn harvest had been even worse than during the Great Hunger. That winter of 1879 – 1880 there was hunger, but not so many deaths. During the Great Famine, it was only the potato crop that had failed. The harvest of all the other crops was grand, but we were not allowed to eat them. The harvested crops were either owned by The Landlord or were used to pay the leases to The Landlord. That was why there was widespread starvation: the people were only allowed legally to eat the potatoes. The rest of the crops were to be shipped out. That winter of 1879-1880 was lean because the harvest had been so poor, but somehow we got past it. I was pregnant with Paul, our sixth child. We found food in unusual places. The four weans and I gathered dulse from on the rocks at the seashore. We collected winkles and barnacles at low tide. Paddy was able to catch a few fish at Culdaff Beach. Uncle Hughie and Auntie Mary, in Boston, sent some money back home to me whenever they could.

Paddy and I had the milk cow and a half dozen hens that were good layers. Most mornings I would find six fresh eggs among the nests in the barn when I went to milk the cow. Mammy taught me to leave a bit of milk in a dish for the hens to keep them from eating their own eggs.

Mammy said, "If the saucer of milk does not stop the egg eating hens, add black pepper to beaten eggs and pour the mixture on the floor when you feed them their grain. That will cure them for sure."

Although we never suffered with that problem with our little flock, I was able to share that wisdom with Susannah.

Chapter 16

The Shirt Factory
1880

he shape of women's lives changed during my lifetime. Perhaps the biggest change occurred with the coming of the shirt factory to Carn. The building was built at the bottom of Bridge Street. Women and girls became seamstresses. Those who were not married would run the machines in the factory and the rest of us would sew the collars and cuffs in our own homes by hand. The girls in the factory would then attach them to the shirts. A woman called the shirt examiner would come around each week to see that the finished shirts were perfect and to give us another dozen shirts to sew for the next week.

It was the first time in our history that women could make a bit of money and that changed us. We could buy more fabric to make clothes; we could buy a greater variety of foods. Some women began to purchase ready-made clothing for their families or a few ornaments for the house. In the years before, only useful things were bought for the house; anything else would be extravagant. After the shirt factory came to Carndonagh, I even had two cook-pots!

In July 1883, I knew that I was increasing again the same way women have known through the ages. A sluggishness of waking in the morning, a feeling of anticipation countered with a bone-weariness that no amount of sleeping will rid the body of. A baby was coming near Christmas. I had been feeling so poorly the previous couple of months. I just figured that it was the remembering.

The previous month in June we had baby Bernard's anniversary. He struggled to live those few days. Our Maggie said that he was not meant for this world. She had said it to help, but even still these many years later, I do still think of what he would be doing, and wonder who he would have looked like.

That July when I knew I was increasing again I realised that if he were still here, Bernard would have been walking, calling me Mammy and getting into everything. I wondered if he would have been funny like John or so serious like Philip. It is very hard losing weans. Every house has its own share of loss. I know that I am not alone in my sorrow. When little Mary died before Philip was born, it was so sudden. She came in for her tay, looking flushed. She sat down beside me and laid her wee hand on my knee.

"I is awful tired, Mammy," she said.

I hugged her to my bosom, laughingly scolding her for running in the fields for too long that afternoon and to my horror, I felt the fever.

The McGuinnesses across the field had lost two children to the fever just the week before. I had tried to keep her from them. I scolded meself, I had not been diligent enough, had she gone into that house? She was so lively, so quick. Nothing escaped her notice. A few days before, she had asked me why Mrs. McGuinness was crying. Maybe she had gone over the fields. I had done everything possible to protect my wean, there was nothing else I could do. The next morning she was gone. She was just three years of age. We buried her in the churchyard next to her Granny. I remember wishing that I had my Mammy to talk to during that time. I was so young to have to experience such grief.

We laid baby Bernard in the ground next to her those nine years later. It is some comfort to me still knowing that they are together and that my Mammy is caring for both of them. I was so afeared that year after Bernard's anniversary with the coming wean.

It was to be my eighth child, two were already gone. I was 36 years old and it was not as easy bringing weans into the world as it was for the first ones. Paddy did not know about the coming wean for a long time. I had told Susannah when I had figured it out, so as we both could feel a bit of joy, but it was not until he asked me the end of September if I was increasing that I finally told him. I was already six months gone at that time.

Chapter 17

The Stations
Spring 1885

Paddy received word from our curate Father Philip O'Doherty, one Sunday after Mass, that we would be having the stations in our house in two weeks time. This was our opportunity to have mass said in our house. There was much to be done in preparation. The two weeks' notice barely gave us enough time to complete the work. The yard needed to be put right, the byre and barn cleaned out and the turf shed organised. The walls were whitewashed with lime from the kilns at the top of Ballyloskey and we painted the front door and the window sills a beautiful bright red. I had hoped to have some flowers blooming even though it was a late spring that year, so I was not confident that I would have flowers.

The girls and I had the job to ready the inside of the house. Even though it was a bit early in the year, we used the stations as a good reason to do our usual thorough spring cleaning that we commonly did annually in May. It was expected that our home would be spotless for the Priest to come and say Mass, since that meant that Our Lord would be present in our home.

We thoroughly scrubbed the walls and the flagstones. The windows were polished. Clothes were cleaned and shoes polished. All the bedding needed to be washed. We took the soap that we had made along with the bedclothes, the feather beds and blankets, down to the wee stream in the middle of the lower field by the landlord's road. We called it the washing stream. I do not know if it had another name.

There are large boulders next to the stream to sit upon and brace yourself while washing the heavy blankets and bedding. This particular stream comes out of the ground with a strong force and goes back underground after about fifteen or twenty feet. The force of the water makes it easy to thoroughly wash and rinse the heavy blankets and beds. The water is so very cold that your feet and hands turn red quickly, but as I always told the weans, if you are scrubbing fiercely enough, you will hardly notice the cold.

The lye soap made from the fire ash is very strong and does irritate the skin, but helps keep the bedbugs away so the discomfort during the washing is worth it. When the blankets and feather beds are clean, we put them on the hedges (the hawthorn bushes that grow alongside the stream) to dry. These bushes are a bit prickly so even the youngest wean learned to stand back a bit and throw the bedding onto the bushes, so as not to be pricked on your hands and arms. The bushes did hold onto the bedding even with the fierce wind we commonly have here. Of course, it is easier to dry them on a sunny day, but the wind will still dry them even on a cold day. Everything was always so fresh when we took it all back into the house and made up the beds again.

Everyone tried to make their houses be the best they could for the stations. When the Priest arrived to say the mass, it was our belief that we were welcoming Our Lord into the house. It was an exciting time and all were delighted to be able to prepare the home for the Lord. The whole family worked together with much anticipation for the coming event.

I do remember when I was a small wean that my parents were cleaning up in preparation for the stations. They were not held as often back then. At the time, the Priests were still a bit wary about attracting attention to the celebration of the Mass. Although Catholic Emancipation had occurred in 1829 and our chapel had been built in Carn shortly after that, the memories of the persecutions of the Penal Laws and the necessity of the Mass Rocks were still very strong among the clergy when I was young.

Since back then the stations were held so infrequently, a couple would only expect to have the opportunity once in their lifetime. My parents keenly felt the importance of preparing for this opportunity. It seems that when someone is denied freedom to act according to their own conscience, when that freedom is restored to them, it is that much more precious.

Mammy often said that it was a grand day when the land was donated just outside of the town for the chapel and graveyard. At the time the law was that Catholic churches were to be built of wood, away from main roads and at least one mile out of the town. The stringent enforcement of the Penal Laws was dependent on the local magistrates, with some more rigorous and others more liberal. We are blessed that our stone chapel is just down the brae from the Diamond on the Derry Road.

In my day it had become much more of a tradition to hold the stations annually. Two or three families in the parish were given the honour of having the stations in their home each year. The Priest comes and your family gathers together, with the neighbours coming in to have Mass in the house. It always brought such a special feeling to see the Priest standing in his vestments in my own home, with the candles set out on my kitchen table next to the Holy Chalice and one of my sons acting so solemn as the altar boy. The Priest was always good to give the boys the special instruction ahead of time as to what their duties were during the Mass.

I cannot adequately describe the feeling that always came over me during the stations. It was not just when the bells were rung and the Priest held the Eucharist up in the air for us all to

103

kneel before. It was also that the Holy Gospel was read out loud in my home. It was hearing the prayers said and participating in the responses uttered. To humbly recognize with my head bowed, that the Lord himself had been in my own home. This special feeling would continue there for weeks afterwards, as in my mind I could hear the words of the Priest blessing us for our faith.

Chapter 18

The Music Left
4 April 1890

ver the winter of 1889-1890, Susannah kept mentioning that Big Shan was making plans to join their children out in Oregon. They were married when I was ten years old and always seemed to me to be so wise. Paddy and I had benefitted many times over the years as we took their counsel. So we did not understand what they were thinking. She was 55 and he was 62. What would make them leave the comforts of home and travel halfway around the world to an unknown place? They planned to travel for over three weeks with five children aged eighteen to seven. It did not make any sense to us, but Big Shan got it set in his mind that they were going. So they made arrangements.

In the early spring, I became aware that I was increasing again. A couple of weeks later, I started having some pains, and I feared that I was losing the baby. The handy-woman came in and gave me some Guelde Rose leafs to stop the pains. I was to brew them into a tea twice a day and to stay in my bed for a few weeks. I never had any trouble before with carrying a wean, so I still wonder if it was the pain of losing Susannah that brought me to my bed. I just could not bear to go down to her house to help with the packing up. Their children and ours were in and out of my house every day with the current report of what was done and what was left to do.

Near the end of March, I was much improved and had no more excuses to stay away. I went down the road to see what was still needed doing. Their big night was arranged for Thursday night and they were to be away on the Friday morning. Word came Thursday morning that the ship, the Buenos Ayrean was delayed arriving into port, and the departure would be one week later on the 4th of April. Everyone came to Ceili that night even though they were not leaving for another week. It was a great night and we all decided to have another party the next week.

I kept a smile on my face that whole week. When I would catch Susannah looking wistfully about the place, I distracted her with stories of Oregon that my girls had written. It was hard going, but there was no sense having her last week be so sorrowful. Big Shan's and Susannah's second Big Night was even better than the first. Friends and relations began gathering at their house about sunset. Food and drink seemed to magically appear on the table with chairs and stools multiplying around the room. Everyone had a place to sit on or lean against. After some time of visiting and carryon, Susannah nodded to her husband. He stepped to the mantle over the hearth and took down his fiddle for the last time. A hush of anticipation settled over the crowd. It was as if we all realised that this was a moment never to be repeated. There we all sat, most of us looking at the flagstones on the floor as the mournful sound of "The Derry Air" slowly wafted around our heads.

When he was finished, he breathed a big sigh and looked around the room. I could not look up. We all just waited to see what would happen next.

Then Paddy said, "How 'bout a lively jig, Shan, we need a bit of a dance now."

The melancholy spell was broken. A tin whistle and bodhran joined the fiddle and we all stood up to dance. I wondered who would play the tunes after Shan had left. How I would miss them all.

Sometime a little before sunrise, Paddy and I went back up the road to begin our morning chores. We hurried through the feeding and milking and tidying up, so that we would not miss the leaving. Paddy went on ahead of me to help Shan with the last minute packing, as I gathered the children to walk down.

As we walked back down the brae to their house, Paul noted that the sun was just up above the horizon over Culdaff Bay. It was a beautiful spring morning, the dew glistening on the leaves of the ditches, birds singing in the trees, the fresh smell of the breeze, but I did not want to find joy in any of that.

When we approached the house, I noticed that Paddy and Shan stood near to one another, silent, in the midst of the hullabaloo of the final packing up. That was their way. I noticed that Nellie's trunk had been loaded onto the wagon. Poor Nellie - Shan and Paddy's sister - had died just before her wedding day a few years before we were married. Her betrothed had made a lovely trunk for her as a wedding present. He was so overwrought with his grief that he would not take back the trunk. He insisted that it remain with the family. Now it was going to America.

I looked inside the cottage. Susannah was trying to brush the floor with the broom a final time, while brushing away the tears flowing down her cheeks. I walked over to her and gently took the broom from her hand, setting it to the side.

"I will tidy the cottage for ye. The McGuinnesses will know what a good housekeeper ye were. It will give me something to do after ye are gone," I said.

She slowly nodded in agreement.

Finally Shan spoke to Paddy. "Ye know there is a fair bit of turf still in the shed. See that ye use it."

"Oh, and Mulherin was to come for those two cows in the byre yesterday. Will ye see that he gets 'em. He has already paid me for 'em. He just needs to collect 'em."

Shan's John said, "We need to go Daddy. We do not want to miss the boat. The wagon is loaded with all our trunks. We just need to get on with it."

Susannah looked over to me. We stepped to each other and silently we embraced. Both of us knew it would be the last time. It was as if time stopped and everything stood still. Although we were not blood, we were very close, especially since the time my Mammy had died.

I felt as if my heart was breaking. She had been my sister, my neighbour, my teacher, my guide, my friend. Over the years, we had laughed and cried and gossiped and worked alongside one another. It seemed that half of me was being ripped away.

We stood there hugging and swaying, silently keening within our minds as our families looked on. Finally Paddy cleared his throat, the spell was broken and we stepped apart. I looked down at the ground, pulling meself emotionally together.

Taking a deep breath, I said, "Write as soon as ye arrive. Give all our relations our regards. Be sure to wear your hat in that hot Oregon sun."

Paddy and I stood there in front of their house as they loaded up in the wagon and urged the horse out into the road. We waved to them until they turned the corner to the right and headed down the brae between the ditches and were out of sight. I told the children to come along. We turned and walked up the road to our cottage and resumed our lives. We never talked about the ache in our hearts that continued to linger.

Our son Philip followed Paddy's brother, Big Shan, and his family the year after they went out to America and the music left our home as well.

Philip was as musically talented as his Uncle Big Shan. My eldest son could pick up and play any instrument, but it was usually the fiddle or the accordion he chose. Shan was the first one to tell us of our Philips' innate ability. It was at the time I was birthin' John. The women were helping me whilst Paddy and Shan were entertaining all the weans at Shan's house. Philip was not yet four years of age. Shan was playing the fiddle and Paddy the bodhran as customary.

Philip stood a short distance away just observing his uncle play. When Shan set the fiddle down to smoke his pipe, young Philip stepped forward and picked up the instrument. Paddy started to correct the wean, but Shan shook his head, as if to say, " just wait to watch and see what happens."

Philip held the fiddle in his left hand and carefully placed it on his neck, tilting his head to the side as he had seen Shan do. As he picked up the bow that was sitting there, he noticed his Daddy and uncle watching.

He started to put the fiddle back down, but Shan, encouraging him, said, "Naw, go on. Let us see how ye do."

Philip solemnly reset the instrument on his neck, placed the fingers of his left hand around the neck and struck the strings with the bow. He actually made some pleasant noise. Paddy said that everyone laughed, but Philip was enthralled. From that moment on he was picking up every instrument that anyone would let him try.

Although Paddy never let on that he was proud of his first-born son's talent, he always made sure that the boy had music lessons from Eugene Canny in Carn from the time he was young. The arrangement was to trade Eugene a load of cut and dried turf each year for the lessons. Philip never did seem to know that Paddy was paying for the lessons and I think that my son believed that Eugene Canny liked him so much, he was pleased to teach him.

Paddy never talked to Philip about his music and Philip never felt like he had his father's support. The two of them never seemed to understand each other. Paddy had lived his entire life under the Penal Laws, with the constant fear of raised rents or evictions. Through the Land Laws passed by the government in the few years previous to Philip's leaving, it became possible for local farmers, such as ourselves, to purchase their leases. Paddy longed to own the land he had been born on.

Paddy believed that the land was more important than any man's personal desires and Philip had dreams that were bigger than Ballyloskey. I think that is why he was so anxious to leave home when he was just sixteen. In addition to his music, Philip was a fine horseman and an eloquent speaker. Out in Oregon, he would play for the country dances in Morrow County to make a little extra money.

Chapter 19

I Become A Granny
8 May 1894

O ur Kate sent us a telegram from Oregon.

"Granny and Granda, Mary Louise Doherty has been born on the 8 May 1894. All are well. Letter to follow."

Reading that telegram, I had such a mixture of feelings. I was so excited to be a granny and yet this small wean, named after me, would grow up so far away without knowing her granny, me. My heart was filled with pride in my daughter and her husband working so hard and now starting a family, but I longed to nestle the baby in my arms and touch her soft cheeks and kiss her tenderly. I folded the telegram and tucked it into my sleeve, and took it out often to reread over the next few weeks until the letter arrived.

Mary was a sweet baby, the letter said, and she hardly made a fuss. Kate was tired for the first few days after the birth, but she said that she recovered quickly and looked forward to having many more children. I still felt that sadness sometimes when I would think about my grandchildren so far away in Oregon, growing up without a close connection to their granny.

Over the next few weeks, I began to realise that there was a way that they would know about me. Since I had learned how to be a mother from my Ma and in turn Kate learned that from me, wee Mary Louise in Oregon would learn of me through the actions of her mother. Every day she would see a bit of me as she watched Kate. That was a comfort. It still was a sad thought that would pierce my heart when I would see the grannies around me cuddling their grandbabies and my arms were so empty.

Chapter 20

Anne's Wedding
29 December 1896

I received a letter from Anne that she wrote before her wedding. She had her wedding suit made and was so excited to wed. She promised to send a photo of her wedding day. It was lovely when it arrived and I did enjoy seeing them all at the party, but I was sad to be missing all of the preparations.

It was great to know that she had her sister Kate there to help her get her things together, but it was hard to miss out on all the craic. It was a little easier for me than when Kate got married three years before. The letters do help and Anne was so good at letter writing that it was as if I had witnessed the events myself when she wrote of them.

Anne married Eddie Doherty from Gleneely. We had heard that there was some serious trouble and accusations by his brother before Eddie was leaving for America. Eddie was given the blame for a tragic accident between his pregnant sister-in-law and the cow she was milking. He left quickly under a dark cloud.

It is sad that there can be such problems between family members. As I read her letter, I hoped that he would make our

Annie a good husband. She was such a gentle soul and so kind to others.

The photograph arrived later in the spring. The wedding had been held in the hotel in Heppner, Oregon. We recognized our own children, of course, Anne, Philip and Kate. Paddy's nephews Phil and Dan Hirl and Lame Barney were in the photograph as well as his niece, Kate Callahan, who had married Eddie's brother Little Barney the year before. There were many others that we had never known what they looked like before, but we had come to know them through letters we received. There was Eddie, the groom, his nephew Ed McDaid, our Kate's husband, James, his sister Mary and her husband, Mike Kenny.

The photograph became more precious to me than anything. I felt like I had seen a little part of my children's life in America. It was wonderful to see that Kate looked especially well, considering that she had just recently been delivered of her third child, Nora. I wished that the new baby had been in the

Wedding Picture of Anne and Ed Doherty, Heppner, Oregon 1896

photograph, but I was grateful to see who was there.

After Anne's wedding, each time a letter would come from one of the children, full of stories and events in their lives, I would take the photograph down from above the hearth and look again at the faces of the people as we read the stories of their lives.

Chapter 21

Our John Leaves
1898

e were used to the delay in getting the news from Oregon, but after our John left with his cousin Ellen for America, it seemed as if we would never hear of their safe arrival. We finally received word from Kate that John had arrived in Blackhorse Canyon and all was well.

They had an epic journey. From the beginning it almost seemed ill fated. Paddy's niece Teresa was to travel out with John, but at the last minute she decided she was not going. She would not be moved, even with all the preparations, the clothes prepared, her trunk packed and the ticket bought. She refused to go, so her younger sister Ellen went in her place. Although they were cousins, Ellen and John signed on as brother and sister, so that they could travel together and not be separated on the ship.

Within a day of leaving Derry City, Ellen took sick. Then they went through a terrible storm at sea. She later wrote her mother that there were a few times during the journey that she thought she would literally die, or at least she wished that she would. They were down in the steerage, in the bottom of the ship and were not allowed up onto the decks, but the sailors in the boiler room enjoyed John's company and he was invited to work with them there. The boiler room crew had sympathy for how sick Ellen was, so they sent down oatmeal gruel for a few days to help her regain her strength.

They sailed into the New York City harbor and Ellen said that the thrill of seeing land again after so rough a crossing caused all the passengers to weep, even the men. They made their way by train across America and finally arrived in Oregon. It took great courage and fortitude to leave one's home and travel halfway around the world to start a new life.

Chapter 22

A Fair Day
22 May 1899

The day began early on 22 May 1899. The pastels of the sunlight filled the eastern sky above the hills at about five in the morning. Although the frost had gone, the dew left her glistening jewels on the ground and bushes, dampening my dress and wetting my feet as I emerged from the house to empty the chamber pot. There was so much to do in this early morning. It was the spring fair day.

The weans could barely sleep the night before in anticipation of the outing. I quieted them finally by threatening that I was perfectly willing to stay at home on the morrow and finish cleaning out the cottage for the day, rather than spoiling such ungrateful children as they were by spending the day in Carn at the fair. Unless they were immediately asleep, there would be no special day for them. The threat accomplished its work: I only heard one or two more giggles in the night after that pronouncement. Truth be told, I was just as excited as my girls.

My granny told me of times, when she was a girl, that the Carn fair days were the great events of the year, not only for the sale of animals, but also for social gatherings, fun and frolic.

Held four times a year, these fairs were a time for games and races, pleasure and amusement, as well as eating and feasting.

The village would be so full you could not pass by on the street. There were always vendors with stalls lining the footpath and animals tied to posts along the way. With children running to and fro, men standing in groups, and women hailing one another across the way, and she said the noise was deafening. As a wean, I could picture a group of musicians attracting a crowd with a variety of tinkers hawking their wares. I would sit and listen at my Granny's knee and just imagine all the wonderful events.

The Carn fair has changed even since I was a girl. It still is a wonderful day out, although there are fewer people about. So many have gone, their memory lingers, but America beckoned. It was on special days like fair days that I missed our eldest children out in Oregon the most. They had moved on with their lives and had families of their own. On those mornings, I wondered if they would even mind the day, that it was the fair day.

Kate, our eldest, probably did. I know that she told the stories to her children, the stories that I wished I could tell to them. I would shake my head, to evict the sadness of separation, and instead turned my face toward the events of the day.

I woke the wee girls and set them to preparing the breakfast and straightening the cottage. They were quick to obey. Everyone silently anticipated leaving for Carn, a bright spot in our usual morning chores. Finally everything was prepared. The animals tended, chores finished, everyone washed and we left. Paddy took the horse and wagon with the eggs and milk for sale, but the girls and I wanted to walk.

The sun was fully visible in the sky by the time we left our farm. Walking down the road we greeted our neighbours, the McCarrons, as they were packing their cart to go to town. Mary McCarron was known for her very fine butter and I asked her to hold some back for me, in case I missed her later in the day.

She laughed and reassured me that she already had me taken care of and to see her on our way back home in the evening. It usually did not take long to walk down the Ballyloskey Road to Carn, but on a fair day, when the streets were clogged with horses and traps, with children and dogs running through the crowd, the trip seemed to take all morning.

The year before in 1898, the Derry Journal described our fair.

"Carn fairs are held quarterly and are 'big days' in the lives of the farming community. At these fairs, horses, cattle, sheep and pigs, together with oats, potatoes and other articles of farm produce, as well as butter, eggs, fish and fowl, are offered for sale. Servant boys and girls can also, as a rule, be engaged at these markets but not in such numbers as in Strabane or Letterkenny."

In our house, we were lucky. None of our weans were sent out to work from these hiring fairs. In many poor families, children as young as six or seven would be hired out for six months at a time for wages to be paid to their fathers. It was a desperate way for the family to have the children fed while trying to gather the money together to pay the land rents. Many times the children were housed in the barns with the animals and were barely fed enough food to survive.

We would see them standing together early on the fair day mornings, in the Diamond, with their fathers or mothers waiting for a farmer to approach and ask, "Are these for hiring"? or the child directly, "Are ye for hiring"?

Often a father would be bold and ask a passing farmer if there was any chance of a job. The children would be standing with a parcel, a sort of code to the farmers that they were available for hire. The parcel might contain a change of clothes and some food. Boys might have some tools and girls might have aprons, but often the parcel was just an old shirt tied together with string, containing nothing, because there was nothing to spare.

Sometimes the farmer would even examine the boys physically, testing them for strength and to see if they were in good health. After the examination, then the bargaining and the interview would begin. It was unnerving and humiliating for the weans. The hiring was finalised by a mutual gesture of slapping hands, the same gesture that was used with the buying and selling of livestock. Farmers then demanded some personal item as security against the workers promise to return later in the day and the young person was free to enjoy the fair for the rest of the day.

It was also customary in our area for the farmer to give the parents a small guarantee of cash that the deal was secure. This was called an earnest or an earl. This pledge was thought of as a legal bond representing the contract for work. After enjoying the fair day, the children would return to the appointed place at the appointed time and climb up into the back of the cart and head off with the farmer. The ride would often be boring and rough and the day would mark the beginning of a period of isolation and separation from their roots and family. There were some farmers who, though they worked their labourers hard, were not deliberately cruel to them.

The McLaughlins across the road usually went down to the Letterkenny hiring fair in May and returned with one or two children to work for the six month term through the summer. They were not cruel to the children. The girls were provided a bed in the house, and they received plenty of food to eat. They worked hard, milking the cows and helping with the farm work. On Sundays, after chapel they were free to do as they pleased.

For about four years running the McLaughlins hired the same girl, Anne Curran from near Raphoe. She came every year from the time she was about 10. Paddy's niece Annie "Callaghan" was six months older and our Anne was six months younger. The three Annes spent their free time together. Our girls thought that Anne's life was a great adventure. To them it seemed exotic and exciting to be hired out. Anne Curran was a hard working girl. She was also very bright, and I have often

122

wondered what happened to her in her life after she was no longer hired out to the McLaughlins.

On that Carn fair day, as was our usual custom going to town, we stopped at the bottom of Mill Brae. Sitting on the rocks by the river's edge, we washed our feet before putting on our shoes to continue on into Carn. It was near to ten that morning, when we finally walked past the chapel and headed up the hill to the Diamond in the center of town.

There was some worry over the previous weeks that a recent influenza outbreak would spoil the day, but folks braved the situation or threw caution to the wind and came out anyway. It seems that everyone was in town. The noises of the cattle and sheep almost drowned out the kenters shouting from their stalls, in an attempt to attract potential buyers for their wares. It was exciting confusion. We saw a couple of old women with their baskets on their arm, going from stall to stall trying to find the bargains.

Both Nora, aged 12, and Sara, aged 11, did not want to stay by my side. Their girlfriends from school stood patiently waiting while I instructed the girls to meet up with me after an hour's time, just over at Canny's hotel, and to mind themselves.

So I was left with Rosie, who was eight, and Maggie, seven. Their eyes were big as saucers. Both of the girls were hesitant to step out from behind my skirts, although their curiosity kept them looking around in every direction at all the commotion. Since we only come to town a few times a year, both of the weans were in awe.

I mind having that same feeling on my first fair day. I do not know how old I was, but Mammy had decided at the last minute to take me with her. It must have been a fair day, but I only knew that I was going to town. Mammy kept hold of my hand on the street but when we opened the door and stepped down into Maguire's shop, she let me go. Mrs. Maguire was standing behind the counter. She stepped out to greet Mammy; they had been at school together. I was not very tall, so I could barely see over the counter top. The stacks of linen and wool on the shelf at the back had drawn Mammy's attention and I was left to wander. I stood for a while and looked about the shop.

So many things, bits and bobs, that I wondered who would buy it all and then where would Mrs. Maguire get more. I then noticed a wee basket in the corner. A lovely white cat lay sleeping. I had never seen a cat inside before. As I hesitantly moved toward her, she awoke and stretched. She mewed and stood up, cocking her head, she invited me to pet her.

I looked up at Mammy; she was not looking, so I stretched out my hand to touch the cat. Just to my left, I heard a door creak and I jumped back, cowering a bit, hoping that no one had noticed my boldness.

As I turned to look, the door swung open and I got a glimpse of the back room. I had no idea that such a world existed behind the back door of the store. Light streaming through a window at the back of the house revealed the scene.

There was a table in the center of the room, with four chairs pulled up to it. Next to the pitcher and bowl placed on the table, a vase of roses caught my eye. I had only seen flowers on their plants and I wondered what they were doing there in the kitchen.

I think that I sighed because Mammy just then noticed what I was doing and firmly called me over to her. I kept on trying to look around her long black skirt to catch another view of that fascinating back room behind the store.

Later I learned that the family lived in the rooms behind the store and I had seen their kitchen. Until then it remained a magical place, a place where extra chairs sat around the table and flowers were put in a glass for enjoyment. That morning was the first time I realised that people lived differently than we did up the Ballyloskey Road.

For our family, the agricultural show was the highlight of the day. Paddy had entered his best sheep in the show, and I had entered a jumper that I had made up for Maggie. The pattern had turned out particularly nice. Sarah had entered a lace handkerchief that she finished in the small clothing section and I had also convinced Paddy to enter the wee wooden animals that he carved into the woodworking section. They were of great proportion and had such intricate detail, that he won a prize. He said that it was nothing, but I could tell that he was chuffed.

Sometime after seven in the evening, I took the girls on back up to the house. They were all exhausted from their day out and were beginning to complain and fight with one another. Paddy stayed on in Carn. I thought that he would be coming up after a few hours. The sun set about half nine and by half ten it was pitch black outside. Still no Paddy. I was beginning to worry when I heard a large ruckus outside the cottage. It was someone running towards the house. I peered out the window, but it was too dark to see anything. I was afraid. I was alone in the house with the girls and no man about. I had nothing with which to defend myself.

I was trying to think about what I could do, when the door burst open and there stood Paddy, lathered up and huffing like a great work horse.

I exclaimed, "What are you on about, you scared me half to death."

He could barely catch his breath.

"The pigs…"

"Came out…"

"From under the bridge…"

"A drove of little…"

"Black pigs chasing…"

"me up the brae" He sat down and collected himself.

"I made it safe. Running as fast as I could, but they almost got me."

I looked out the window. I could not see anything. It was so dark that night. I could tell that he had enjoyed himself a little too much at the fair. Later when he recounted the story of the little black pigs chasing him, I suggested that perhaps he had been a little drunk. He assured me that his consumption of alcohol had nothing to do with it. He was convinced that he had been attacked by a drove of pigs down by the bridge over

Ballywilly Brook and had barely made it home alive. It seemed that after that, on many a fair day, late at night, those same little black pigs plagued him on his way home to us. I tried not to laugh when he would come home with this story.

Chapter 23

St. Mary's School
1900

In the dark mornings of winter, I would hear the children creep down the stairs. They would try not to disturb my sleep in those cold moments just before the dawn. The turf fire had almost gone out. The embers just needed a wee bit of stirring and a couple of new pieces of turf to restore the heat, but the cold and damp of the morning would sometimes keep me within my bed if I was feeling poorly and I would wait for one of the children to come into my room to rebuild the fire. After their chores, they ate their breakfast of porridge and headed down the road to school.

During the early Penal times, educating Catholics was outlawed,

"No person of the popish religion shall publicly or in private houses teach school, or instruct youth in learning within this realm' upon pain of twenty pounds fine and three months in prison for every such offence."

This law was repealed in 1782, but the effects continued to be felt in local communities for years.

In order to educate the children local communities employed teachers, called Masters, to teach their children in an informal system called Hedge schools. The level of education given to the children depended on the ability and qualifications of the particular Master. Many children were given a classical education that rivaled the best schools.

Unfortunately, in some areas, the Masters were not good educators and the children were illiterate. When my parents were young, everyone spoke Irish. As a child, we spoke Irish in our home and with our neighbours, but at school we were taught to read and write English and were expected to use it. By the time Paddy and I were rearing our children, although we had some Irish phrases we would use in everyday life, our communication was all in English and now it seems as though our Irish is lost.

I have heard of some communities in West Donegal and down in Galway that are holding on to the old ways. The new government wants all children to learn Irish in school, but first the district supervisors need to teach the teachers Irish before those teachers can teach the children. In 1832, when Mammy was still a young girl, the British government decided that education was to be freely given to all children and the National schools were built around the country. It did not matter who your family was, what your religion was or where you lived, all the children were to be educated.

The National Schools gave children a well rounded education. In the small two story school house down the lane next to the chapel, we mastered Gough's arithmetic, learned about cube and square root as well as the simpler rules of subtraction, addition and multiplication. We read *Cook's Geography*, Sir Walter Scott and Dickens, and other books like *Robinson Crusoe*. I thoroughly enjoyed reading the "Lady of the Lake" more than once.

Our old school is no longer used for teaching children and is now called the Wee Hall. The Wee Hall is still sometimes used for community events but usually people enjoy the more modern Colgan Hall built across the road from the graveyard. St.

Mary's Convent School was a great blessing to our small community when it first opened in 1900. The nuns had been formally trained as proper teachers in a variety of subjects. They introduced a wider curriculum. In addition to the subjects already in existence, they began to teach manual instruction, drawing, elementary science, singing, cookery, laundry and physical drill.

Typical early 20th century Irish classroom

The headmistress, Sister Mary Rose explained,
"The subjects will no longer be compartmentalised, but rather they will be taught seamlessly in an integrated manner. We will create an environment to stimulate learning and allocate ten minutes every hour for rest and play."

Paddy was appalled. He wanted to withdraw the girls, but since they were enforcing compulsory education until age 14, I suggested that we give it a try and see what happened. I knew that our younger girls were enjoying the new subjects. Rosie especially enjoyed the drawing, while Sarah was excited to improve her singing.

Chapter 24

The Railroad Came
1901

The Londonderry and Lough Swilly Railway began service in 1863, connecting the bottom of the Swilly with Derry City. The following year a line opened to Buncrana. Then the route was re-gauged from the broad gauge to the narrow three inch gauge beginning in 1883 because it was cheaper to maintain.

In 1884 a proposal was made for a link to Carn from Buncrana, however it was rejected the next year by Parliament. Some of the townspeople thought that the coming of the railroad would not only improve the ability to transport the farm products to market, but it might also revive the Carn Fair Day with more visitors coming down for the day. A government study was done in 1897 with the proposal for the railway to expand transport to cattle, in addition to sheep. For the two years after 1897 we heard rumors and stories of government plans to build a narrow gauge railway from Buncrana to Carn.

On the 22 May 1899, Mr. Gerald Balfour, the Chief Secretary of Ireland and his wife Lady Betty Balfour, came to Carn to perform the ceremony of cutting the sod to begin the building of the Carn-Buncrana line. Mrs. Balfour was given a spade of solid silver to perform the turning of the first sod. After cutting the sod, she placed it in a specially built railway barrow of polished elm. She took hold of the barrow and amid loud cheers, she wheeled it down a wooden passage from a slightly raised platform and tilted the sod to the ground. She returned the barrow to its former place, while the band played "The Bluebells of Scotland." Facing the people, Lady Betty declared that the construction of the Buncrana and Carn Railway Extension was now commenced.

After that day, we all watched with great anticipation as the railway bed was carved out of the hillsides and through the fields, in the bog from Buncrana to Carn and then on to Ballyliffin. The rails were laid and the station house was built down below the town along the Malin road. Everyone wondered what changes the railroad would bring to the town. With the faster overland transportation of goods we speculated that the haberdashery would have the newest fashions sooner. Because it would be cheaper to send goods by rail than overland coach we all wondered if we could expect a greater variety of items to choose from in the local shops.

Would the greengrocer have different vegetables and fruits than what we grew in our local area? Would there be some things that we had never heard of before? Perhaps there would be more than one selection of lampshade for the oil lamp or one choice of ready-made soap for our Saturday's bath day.

The Carn line was finally finished and opened on 1 July 1901. I walked down to the station house with the girls to watch all the excitement. At half eight that morning, the first train from Derry City arrived at Carn station. All of us who had made the effort to witness the train's arrival in Carn had to stand behind the fence next to the tracks. William Lawrence, a famous photographer, came all the way up from Dublin to capture the event, but there was not much of a crowd. I did think that it was exciting to see the great engine with its carriages, lumbering up to the station house. Paddy was glad that he had stayed home to work in the fields.

132

The Carn line is special. Not only is it part of the fastest narrow gauge rail system in the world, it has a ghost train. The phantom train has made three appearances on the line at Kinnego Halt. It consists of an engine, two carriages and a brake van. The story is that the gate keeper, on hearing the lonesome whistle of the train and thinking that an unscheduled special was coming through, rushed to open the gates, but before he could do so, the mystery train passed through the unopened gates unhindered and disappeared into the mist. It has reportedly been seen near Buncrana as well.

Over the two years it took to build the railway line, it had been great fun to talk about what the future would hold. Progress was coming to Carn. Everyone hoped that letters and newspapers would arrive quicker, for the news was sometimes weeks old before we heard of it in the northwest of Ireland. We all knew that there would be great inventions and inroads into the modern world and that everything would change because of the railroad.

While those things did happen, I did not anticipate that the railroad would take the young ones away sooner. It was easier for them to make arrangements to leave for England, or America, or wherever they went to seek their fortunes.

One by one my children left. It was so easy, they just had to make it down to Carn and then the train took them to Derry. After that the ships took them to America. Not just our house, but all the neighbours as well. This heartache was in every house. We came to realise that this progress we had been so excited to have just increased our loneliness.

Chapter 25

Photographs
1903

The year that my niece Cassie Marley was living with us, Paddy and I decided to go to Derry City to have our photograph taken. We took the wee girl with us because we were tending her. My sister Maggie and her husband Willie Marley were in Glasgow trying to make their way there. There has been a strong connection between Inishowen and Scotland for as long as anyone can remember. Young men especially would head out on the boats over to Scotland to work the harvests. It was typically seasonal work in the fields.

The workers lived a very frugal lifestyle in order to earn the necessary money to pay the land rents to the Landlords and to buy goods to supplement their marginal existence. They would live in their employers' barns and sheds, and work all the daylight hours, which enabled them to bring more money back to Ireland to really help their families.

Paddy and I had agreed to keep the wean with us for that first year after they left for Scotland. So while Maggie and Willie worked to set themselves up in Glasgow we had Cassie. When they were all ready they returned for her.

135

Cassie was a delightful child and very easy to keep. She was very obedient and was happy looking after herself, playing near me while I worked through the days even though she was only three years of age. She was a beautiful child.

Since our youngest children were practically grown. Maggie was already 11 years old and very independent. I found great delight in looking after a wean again. Maggie and Rosie doted on the child and looked after her like she was a wee doll. Cassie was delighted to follow them around while they were doing their school assignments or chores. She would copy them and try to do whatever they were doing.

For our photograph, we used the items in a package my sister Sarah had sent from Boston with a bit of money, a shawl, a nice skirt and the fanciest hat that I had ever seen. Paddy received a new jacket, waistcoat, tie and collar for his shirt. He looked very smart.

Taking the train from Carn to Derry made it a real special day. We even dressed Cassie up in her best dress to be able to send a photograph of her off to Maggie and Willie. We walked down the road to the river at the bottom of the brae, washed off our feet and put on our shoes as was our usual routine. We walked past the chapel and through the Diamond, down the hill to the station house to purchase our tickets and await the train.

It was coming up from Ballyliffin along Trawbreaga Bay and we could hear the chugga-chugga of the engine a long time before we actually saw it approaching. It stopped at the station house with a huge whoosh and screech. Cassie hid behind my shirts, but peeked around me in anticipation, not sure whether to be afraid or excited. The whistle blew and we got on board with the rest of the passengers.

We had brought Maggie and Rosie along for the day as well. It was easier to bring them along than to have them whinge and whine about missing all the excitement of riding the train to Derry City. I had some money put aside from sewing shirts and we planned to take our dinner in the City Hotel and act as if we were part of the smart set. To sit in the train and watch the hills

136

and glens rolling by the windows was a delight and we all really enjoyed the trip. When we arrived at the Station House in Derry, it was right by the Quay and we made our way up Shipquay Street and into the photography studio.

We did not have an appointment, but the proprietor, Mr. James Glass assured us as we opened the door that we were grand and that he would be with us in a moment. He was bent over a table sorting some photographs. He looked very professionally dressed with his white shirt, starched collar and dark braces holding up his tweed trousers. His dark hair however was terribly tousled and the girls giggled behind their hands as they noticed.

It soon became apparent why his hair was in such disarray as he continually had to climb under the cape over the back of the camera in order to shoot the portrait and then climb back out to set up the next one.

As we were waiting and he was finishing up his sorting he asked us who we wanted in the photograph and how many portraits we wanted taken. It was so expensive to have them taken and Rosie and Maggie were fine with not being in the setup. Paddy and I decided to each have a separate portrait taken. We did have one taken together with Cassie to send on to Maggie and Willie.

Mr. Glass suggested that we start with the three of us so as not to try the child's patience. However, he scared her to death, and she would not stand there with us at all. She ran behind Rosie and said that Uncle Paddy had to be first.

So Uncle Paddy was first. He stood there on his own in front of the painted fabric backdrop. He was so handsome. I wished, years later, that I had kept a copy of the portraits taken that day.

It was hard in those days to take photographs. You had to stand so still and there was a brace that they used to keep you from moving. It would go up the back of your jacket and hold your head, to remind you to stand still. You could not smile or move at all. The photographer said that if we moved the photograph would be ruined. So Paddy looked rather stern in his portrait, but I did notice that if you looked very carefully, you could still see the twinkle in his eye.

Then it was my turn. I was very nervous. Just standing there, it was as if I was shaking and I was sure that the photograph would be ruined. But Mr. Glass was very experienced in calming his subject for the portraits and it turned out all right. I am afraid that I did look rather stern, but it was more from fear than being my character. The shawl and hat were really lovely and I too felt rather smart that day.

Finally Cassie was ready to stand in front of the painted fabric. She saw that we were unharmed from the experience and she had actually begun to be a bit curious about the whole process. Mr. Glass had her stand on a chair between Paddy and myself.

It was difficult for my sister, this time of being separated from her child, even though it was necessary. I know that Maggie really appreciated receiving the portrait. It was a comfort to her to have the portrait while they were getting established in Glasgow. They really appreciated seeing how much she had grown since they had been gone. In her letter back to me after receiving it, she said that she had carried the photograph around with her for a month, just taking it out and looking at it all the time. She missed her wee girl so much.

Paddy decided to order largish copies of the separate portraits of the two of us. Yer man had quite lovely tin frames with curved glass and hard backs that would protect the portraits. They were about two feet in height, and we looked so distinguished, like some of the great folks from the big houses with their portrait galleries.

After he had picked them up a month later in Derry, he was delighted to hang them on the cottage wall in the lower room. We began calling it the sitting room, since we had those fancy portraits hanging on the wall.

It was a hard decision to pack them in Rosie's trunk those many years later, in 1911, when she was heading off to Oregon.

It was right to send them out because most of our family was out there. For some of them it had been over twenty years since they had left and it was good for their children to know who we were and what we looked like.

Over the years, I would often look at the bare walls where they had hung and miss them, but I would remember that Paddy was very handsome that day. Later I was glad that we had the photographs taken so that the ones in Oregon could see how we were getting on.

Paddy had told Rosie to bring the portraits back home with her when she came back. Even up to the day of his death, eight and a half years later, he thought that his Rosie would be coming back home to him.

Mary and Paddy with Niece Cassie in 1903

Chapter 26

Eugene Left
Summer 1905

ugene was born the year after our baby Bernard died. He was spoiled as a child, and catered to. Even when I knew that he wanted to go to America, I hid the fact from Paddy. Eugene never actually said to me that he was leaving, I just knew.

Four years earlier Nora had left home to join the others in Oregon. She was the next younger to him and the look that crossed his face when we read her letters told the story. He did not want to be left behind as all the others had gone.

Without any forewarning, he made his announcement to me after finishing breakfast that morning in the summer of 1905. Paddy had already left to turn the hay in the lower field. Eugene said that he had carefully planned his departure without telling any of the family.

He had purchased a ticket to take the train to Derry and had his passage booked for America. He was going on to Oregon. He decided to leave on the second boat of the season travelling to America in order to help his Daddy with the planting and spring farming. He said that we would be able to handle the rest of the harvest. Nothing I said would change his mind, it was

141

all arranged. They already knew in town at Canny's Hotel to keep the horse and trap. He had told them that we would be down later to collect it.

I was devastated. Smiling with a brave face, I watched him turn the corner at the bottom of the brae. Then when he was out of sight, I collapsed to my knees, almost keening, for it was as if he was dead to me. I knew that I would never see him again. I cried the rest of the day.

It was more than just another one of the weans leaving us for America, as Eugene had left us alone to do the farming and tend the animals: an old man going blind, me with my bad back and the three younger girls. The neighbours would step in and help us when they could, but times were tough. The girls worked hard, but it took them so much longer to do the work around the farm. We could not yield as much from our garden or from the fields as able-bodied men would produce working the farm.

After he returned home at dinner time that day and discovered that Eugene had left, Paddy quit talking directly to me for about a year. Every communication that was needed between us went through Sarah, Rosie or Maggie. I think that was when I first noticed Paddy working his mouth when he was deeply thinking or disturbed about something. He rubbed his lips in wee circles vigorously against one another. It became a sign to us to steer clear until the movement stopped.

He told the girls that he blamed me for Eugene's going away. He said that I should have told him our son was leaving. Paddy did not understand that it was as big of a shock to me as it was to him. Although I suspected that Eugene was planning on going, it was a constant prayer of mine that he would stay.

Gradually Paddy began to talk to me again, but the strain was obvious. One of our boys had to come home from Oregon, someone needed to keep working the land. A few years passed with no relief so finally I wrote to Paul in Oregon without Paddy knowing and asked him if he would return.

In the spring of 1909, Paul came home. He came back because there was no one else. Eugene had just up and left and refused to return. In fact after two years of being in Oregon with the rest, he went up to Fairbanks in Alaska.

As the oldest, it was Philip's duty, but he was already married and had a family. Paul was the one because John would not come home either. John had decided that he was also going to Alaska. When Paul arrived home, he told Paddy that he came home just for a visit. He said that he was going back in a month's time, but I could tell by the way he looked at his da, he was staying.

Eugene's leaving broke my heart and Paddy's spirit. One by one the weans had gone. It was hard on Paddy when we learned of his brother Big Shan's death in Oregon in 1903. It had been 13 years since they went out to Oregon and I know that Paddy missed him daily, but Eugene's leaving was different.

Perhaps it was because we doted on him, perhaps it was because as Paddy was aging, Eugene was doing more and more of the farming. Perhaps it was because he was the only son left at home, but Eugene's careful plan to sneak away broke his father. Paddy never forgave him.

Chapter 27

My Father Died
1905

A week or so after we received a letter from Kate telling us that Eugene had arrived in Oregon, I had another terrible blow. My father, who had been a source of strength and security to me for my entire life, died. He had been out milking a cow in the barn, and feeling poorly, sat down on the stone step just outside the door. My brother Philip was the only one of us still living at home. He heard the cow bellowing and going to investigate the noise, found my father slumped over against the wall.

Father was barely breathing and did not come around as Philip carried him into the house and laid him on his upper room bed. This is where I found them both about an hour later. Father was ashen and grey, struggling to breathe, lying on the bed with Philip a few feet away fidgeting in a chair.

I arrived for my usual morning routine of fixing their meal and tidying the house. I had no idea of the drama that was in front of me that morning as I strolled whistling down the lane to my home place. As soon as Philip saw me, he bolted upright and mumbling something about the cow needing him, he headed for the door.

I had to call his name twice to get his attention, he was so intent on leaving the tragic scene.

"Philip, I said, you must go and get Paddy. Hurry, quick now, go and get Paddy and then off down to the hospital. We need to see if there is anything we can do for our father. The doctor may be able to help him."

As Philip quickly left the house to collect the doctor from the hospital at the Workhouse, I was reminded of the treatment my father had 10 years before when he first took sick. He had been chewing on the dried parsley leaves for a few weeks. It was known locally as a great help with shortness of breath. My granny had always grown parsley in her kitchen garden and so did I. Parsley needs to be planted each year although seeds can be kept for up to five years. It is considered lucky to plant the seeds on Good Friday.

In addition to helping with breathing, parsley is also used to relieve those who suffer from rheumatism or female problems. I do not mind if the parsley was relieving his symptoms at all, but I did notice that it helped sweeten up his breath.

One morning he took a turn, and seemed disoriented and confused, so I brewed some nettle tea. I filled up the kettle with fresh water, brought it to a boil and added two handfuls of dried leaves. After infusing the leaves for 10 minutes, the tea was ready to be strained and used.

My brothers had enjoyed harvesting the nettles when we were young, from mother's kitchen garden in the spring or early summer because they would chase me around the yard, threatening me with the sting. The sting does go away when you dry the plant. Drinking nettle tea is a great cure for many health problems; locals use it in the spring time as a cleanse. After a few days of serving him the tea, I did not feel that father was improving. I worried that it might be his heart and so I told him that we needed to call in the bean chabhhartha, the handy-woman.

146

She was usually called in to help with childbirth and laying out the dead, so he laughed and said that he knew he did not feel well, but he did not think that he was either increasing or dead. I reminded him that she was also called in for various illnesses because of her great knowledge of healing herbs and plants. He agreed, so Mrs. Mary Ann McGuinness was sent for.

Mary Ann looked him over and said that she thought it was his heart. She told me which three plants to prepare and to give to him daily. I listened intently but was surprised at her selections.

Foxglove was known to me as a poisonous flowering plant, yet I was told to create a tincture by putting a half handful of dried berries into a glass pint of spirits. I was to allow it to sit above the hearth for two weeks, shaking every day before transferring it to a dark bottle. She handed me a small dark bottle of tincture she had previously prepared and instructed me to give my father a spoonful each morning until mine was prepared. Next she told me to harvest some horseradish root, dry it and grate it. Taking the horseradish and combining with dried hawthorn berries, I was to make an infusion which I was to give to father two spoonfuls, three times a day.

Hawthorn has small glossy dark green leaves on thorny branches and is commonly used as a thick protective hedge. The beautiful white flowers grow in clusters, usually appearing in May. When the flowers die, the berries gradually appear and are ready to harvest from the end of August. The leaves and flowers need to be dried quickly. Mary Ann told me to harvest them on a dry day and lay them out on a tray near the fire, so that the heat will pull out the moisture. It takes about three days. The berries need to be dried slower. I had some dried hawthorn berries in my press because my mother had taught me to use it as a poultice to draw out thorns and splinters from skin, but I had no idea that hawthorn helped with heart problems.

My granny always said that drinking hawthorn leaf tea kept her from having the flu. She told me that there was not an herb without a cure.

147

For the past ten years, I had prepared the infusion and tincture for father and he took them daily. Mary Ann would call in every once in a while to check on her patient, but he was grand.

Until that day Philip found him sitting just outside the barn.

I silently hoped that there would be another cure, but just looking at father, I just knew that he would be gone by the end of the day. His eyes were glazed over and his colour was so bad. His breathing was laboured, shallow and erratic.

Paddy breathlessly arrived a few minutes later. Philip must have run up to the field and wasting no time, they both ran down to the house, with Paddy bursting through the door first. He first looked at father on the bed and then our eyes met. Without words, his eyes confirmed what I knew to be true. He slowly nodded and together we both looked back at father on the bed, listening for his last breath.

The doctor arrived after a time. I was unaware of how long it had been since Philip left to collect him, so I was a little startled when they returned. The doctor quickly surveyed the situation and told us that it would not be long now and suggested that Philip go and get the Parish Priest. Our father needed to receive Extreme Unction. These last rites are one of the seven Holy Sacraments and every Catholic should receive this Anointing of the Sick if possible. Mammy had not received them all those years ago as she had been found dead that day sitting in her chair by the fire when the younger weans had returned from school.

As a family we were worried about the repose of her eternal soul until the Priest told us that Mammy had been in a state of grace at her death. She had trusted in God all her life, so her sins would be forgiven her even though she did not receive Extreme Unction.

Father John O'Doherty solemnly entered the house and saw that my father was in no condition to receive the Sacraments of Penance and the Eucharist that precede the Sacrament of

148

Unction. Father John explained that he would just begin with the Anointing with the Oil of the Sick.

This olive oil was blessed by the Bishop of Derry on Maundy Thursday (the Thursday of Holy Week). He then asked us to bring a table near the bed and cover it with a white cloth. Father John placed a Crucifix on the table with two blessed candles on either side. The candles were lit. He asked for a dish of water and a clean cloth to wipe his fingers on. He took from his pocket a bottle of holy water and a piece of palm that had been blessed on Palm Sunday. This was used to sprinkle the room with holy water.

Then began the prayer of the Sacrament recited in Latin, *"Per istam sanctan unctionem et suam piissimam misericordiam, indúlgeat tibi Dóminus quidquid per visum, audtiotum, odorátum, gustum et locutiónem, tactum, gressum deliquisti."*

Translated this means,

"Through this Holy Unction or oil, and through the great goodness of His mercy, may God pardon thee whatever sins thou hast committed by sight, hearing, smell, taste and speech, touch, ability to walk."

As he said the prayer, Father John took the oil and anointed my father in the six places corresponding to the prayer: eyelids, ears, nostrils, lips, hands and feet. After anointing each place, he wiped it with a wee piece of cotton. After finishing this Sacrament, Father John told us that our father had received a remission of his sins and that his soul was now prepared to depart this life and receive his eternal reward.

That is when I began to cry. Not the loud wailing keening, the sing-song public display of grieving that is traditional during a wake or a funeral, but the deep and silent grieving of a heart breaking.

If Paddy and I had been all right at the time, or my sisters had been around, or if more of the children had still been at home, I do not think that I would have taken father's death so

149

hard. But as it was, I had never felt so alone and sorrowful as I did sitting by my father's bed waiting in the silence of his impending passing.

Irish traditions surrounding the death, wake and burial of a person may seem strange to outsiders, but they do comfort us. The traditional Irish Wake is commonplace all over Ireland. It is the period of time from death until the body is conveyed to the chapel.

Traditions include the process of laying out the body of a departed relative in the house. A window will be opened so that the spirit of the deceased may leave the room. It is considered bad luck to walk or stand between the deceased and the window, as this is thought to interrupt the progress of the soul out the window. After two hours, the window is then closed to prevent the soul from returning to the body.

The local handy-women who are experienced in handling the body arrive. The deceased is washed, dressed in their best clothes, and covered with a shroud from the chest down, keeping the head and hands visible. If the deceased is a man, he will be clean shaven before being clothed.

A bed is then prepared, and the body is laid out on the bed, settle or kitchen table in the upper room. All clocks are stopped at the time of death as a mark of respect. Mirrors are turned toward the wall, covered or removed because the ghost of the deceased does not want to see itself. A crucifix is placed on the breast and rosary beads are put in the fingers. Sheets are hung around the bed, along two or three sides. Candles are lit in candlesticks and placed near the remains. This process takes about two hours.

Immediately after they prepare the body, the women begin keening. This vocal lamentation sounds a bit like wailing to those who are not accustomed to it. When one keener loses volume, another takes up the cant. Superstition holds that keening must not begin until after the body is prepared or evil spirits will surround the wake and body. Keening continues throughout the wake and later at the graveside.

When all has been made ready, the front door is opened and the family, neighbours and friends begin to gather at the house. During a wake, the front door of the house remains open, almost as a sign inviting all the neighbours and friends to come into the house and pay their respects to the deceased.

There is always a lot of food and plenty of drink to be consumed. Supplies are brought into the house, bread, milk and food of all kinds. Also whiskey, stout, wine, pipes, tobacco and snuff are available. A plate of snuff is passed around for all to take a pinch. Clay pipes filled with tobacco are made available as well. The eldest boy in the house or the son of a close neighbour is given the honour of cutting the tobacco and filling the pipes. When the coffin has been finished by the undertaker, it is placed against the wall near the remains.

Throughout the wake, people socialize and remember the departed person's life. The deceased is never left unattended from death until burial. The news travels very fast over long distances and people come from near and far.

Typically, a wake is attended by family, relatives, neighbours, friends, school friends, as well as acquaintances. One does not have to wait to be invited. Upon entering the house, the mourner makes their way first to the side of the corpse, either kneeling or standing nearby, they silently recite a few prayers for the departed soul. Close relatives will kiss the cheek of the deceased or touch the hands or head with holy water. Then the visitors greet the family and offer some comforting words.

This part of the wake is very solemn and respectful. Shaking hands and expressing sympathy to the family for their trouble, the visitor will speak kindly of the deceased and then moves away from being up at the corpse. Only the best stories of the person are told during the wake. Irish people never speak ill of the dead; the stories are a comfort to the family.

One can expect to see people sitting around drinking tea, eating sandwiches, biscuits and cakes and chatting – even in the room where the body is laid out. Moving to the other end of the room or into the kitchen, the mourner will be offered food and drink during the time spent at the wake. If the weather is good, the men will congregate outside, if not, they will go into the kitchen. Sometimes after sitting in silence for a while, one of the family would start a decade of the rosary up near the corpse, with those in the house reciting the responses. This would pass the time. Mass may also be said in the house.

Most visitors will stay for a few hours and leave by midnight. Close family and neighbours will remain until morning. They drink tea, whisky or beer and talk about general affairs. Anecdotes are told with quiet laughter but within a solemn and decorous mood.

A wake is an integral part of the grieving process for family, friends and neighbours of the deceased. Not commonly a time for tears, it usually is a mixture of sadness and gaiety. Music, dancing, and physical games make the wake feel more like a party. The Priests have tried several times to abolish the consumption of alcohol at wakes.

Though it is a time of sadness, the presence of friends and family makes it more bearable and there is generally great joviality as the deceased is fondly remembered. I know of one family in Glentogher that traditionally will play a game of cards and include a hand for the deceased.

It is the traditional Irish way of celebrating one's life and ensuring that the deceased has a good send off. This tradition is said to originate with the ancient Celts. In their belief system, once someone died in this world they moved on to the afterlife, which was a better world and thus cause for celebration. Burial takes place three days after death.

The saddest moment is when the deceased is leaving home for the last time. The undertaker arrives at the home to place the corpse in a coffin or casket and then with the Priest heading the procession, the funeral begins heading toward the chapel. This is the last time for mourners to commiserate before the casket is closed. A wake is a scene of both sadness and joy as the end of the loved one's life is marked but their life itself is remembered and treasured.

152

After the funeral, all the friends and relations drop by the house and partake of the vast quantities of food and drink that have appeared, as if by magic, into the house. Often, the family will arrive home and find that the house has been cleaned from top to bottom and every surface of the kitchen and beyond is weighed down with the best of food and drink.

There may be tears, but there is plenty of laughter as well, as all the funny stories, happy times, and triumphs of the dead are shared and recorded in the memories of the living.

A Mass and another feast is held one month and then annually after the death. These are called the Month's Mind and Year's Mind or anniversary. These minding days have been Irish traditions for thousands of years. These are the days where deceased souls are held in special remembrance and provide comfort to those who remain.

In an Irish village when a person died, a woman would sing a lament at the wake and funeral. These women singers are sometimes referred to as keeners, from the Irish *caoineadh*, meaning to weep and wail. The tradition of keening over the body is distinct from the wake.

The keen itself has specific elements, such as listing the genealogy of the deceased, praising their virtues and accomplishments as well as emphasizing the woeful conditions of those left behind. The best keeners would be in much demand.

Keening is a loud and wailing, exaggerated and mournful dirge. The words of it are not always articulated, but when they are so, they express the praises of the deceased, and the loss the family or clan would sustain by his death.

Traditions tell us that in ancient times it was the duty of the bard attached to the family of each chief or noble to raise the funeral song. He would be assisted by some of the household of the deceased. Now in our time keeners are hired mourners, who are compensated according to how talented they are.

I remember at my granny's wake when I was just a child, the local woman, Mrs. McDermott, was called in. She was highly regarded because of the vast store of Irish verses she could repeat. Her memory was extraordinary. I was so curious that when the other children were led out of the room, I hid in the corner, behind a chair. In the dim light, no one noticed me crouching in the shadows.

Standing over the corpse, she commenced. She seemed to mumble for a short time, probably the beginning of each stanza, as if to assure herself of their arrangement. Then with her eyes closed, she rocked her body backward and forward and clapped her hands, as if keeping time to the measure of the verse.

She began in a kind of whining recitation, but as she proceeded, and as the composition required it, her voice assumed a variety of deep and fine tones, and the energy with which many passages were delivered, proved her perfect comprehension and strong feeling of the subject. I was mesmerized. At the end of each stanza, those in the room would join in with Mrs. McDermott in a wild and inarticulate uproar of sound, almost as a choir joining in on the chorus.

> "*Silence prevails; it is an awful silence.*
> *The voice of Mary is heard no longer in Ballyloskey.*
> *Yes, thou art gone, O Mary!*
> *but Maggie McDermott*
> *will raise the song of woe, and bewail thy fate.*
> *Snow white was thy virtue; the youths gazed on thee*
> *with rapture; and old age listened with pleasure*
> *to the soft music of thy tongue. Thy beauty was brighter*
> *than the sun which shone around thee, O Mary!*
> *but thy sun is set, and has left the soul of thy friend*
> *in darkness. Sorrow for thee is dumb,*
> *save the wailings of Maggie McDermott;*
> *and grief has not yet tears to shed for Mary.*
> *I have cried over many a rich man;*
> *but when the stone was laid upon his grave,*
> *me grief was at an end. Not so with me heart's darling,*
> *our dear Mary; the grave cannot hide her*
> *from the view of Maggie McDermott.*

I see her in the four corners of her habitation,
which was once gilded by her presence.
O Mary, Thou didst not fall off like a withered leaf,
which hangs trembling and insecure:
no, it was a rude blast which brought thee to the dust!
Hadst thou not friends enough?
Hadst thou not bread to eat, and raiment to put on?
Hadst thou not experienced both youth and beauty, Mary?
Then mightest thou not have stayed with us?
But the spoiler came, and disordered our peace:
the grim tyrant has taken away our only support in Mary!
In thy state of probation, thou wert kind hearted to all,
and none envied thee thy good fortune.
Oh! that the lamentations of thy friends—
Oh! that the burning tears of Maggie McDermott
could bring back from the grave the peerless Mary!
But alas! this cannot be: then twice in every year,
while the virgins of the valley celebrate the birth
and death of Mary, under the wide spreading elm,
let her spirit hover round them, and teach them
to emulate her virtues. So falls into the depth of silence
the lament of Maggie McDermott."

In silence, she slowly lowered herself onto the flagstone floor as we all wept the tears of our grief. Later, I asked Mammy if all the keeners were like unto Mrs. McDermott. She patted me on the head and told me that it was our tradition and it brought great comfort during such a difficult time.

If the proof of a man's goodness is measured by the crowd at his funeral, then my father was indeed a good man. The chapel was filled to overflowing. I could not believe the crowd that had gathered along the way as the remains were carried down Ballyloskey and over to the chapel.

Sometimes funeral processions will be enlarged by the chance meeting with other folks because it is considered unlucky if any person meeting a funeral passes it without turning back to accompany it at least some short distance. But as we walked along the road, I recognized and could name all those who honoured my father by accompanying him on his final journey.

It was a lovely morning of early spring, the trees were rapidly assuming their most brilliant clothing of green and there was a genial warmth in the air. The sun shone brightly, and the lively songs of the birds added their influence which commonly would cheer and comfort me. I reflected that usually this walk on such a day would take my mind to that place where all cares and anxieties of life are utterly forgotten and only the momentary pleasures of a country walk would entertain my thoughts. But for me, that day was not such a day.

The keening of the funeral procession would rise from a sort of a murmur, swelling out into full tones and then die away into silence. Almost as a harp, the voices of the women at the front would gradually rise in strength as the other women joined in. The men occasionally added their deeper tones to complete the melancholy sound.

It might have been the contrast with the joyful sounds of the birds, or just the state of my own mind, but that morning the keening struck me as the most mournful expression of grief that I could imagine.

Six men at a time carried the casket on their shoulders, side-by-side they walked, interlocking their arms under the casket onto the shoulder of the man opposite. Almost un-noticed each man in turn would be relieved by another after a short distance, as our closest male relatives willingly carried my father down.

As we entered the chapel doors, I looked over to my right to the place in the graveyard, already prepared, where my father would be laid to rest. I knew that he was at peace, but I was still so bowed down with grief that I could only recognize my loss.

Chapter 28

A New House
1909

Paul began preparations to build himself a new house almost as soon as he landed home. He had brought a bit of money back from America with him and he hired Big Denny Salty who was McLaughlin to do the building. Big Denny Salty first removed the topsoil from the area that Paul had selected for the new house at the end of our house. Then he dug a rectangle trench the size of the house, about two feet deep to create the foundation. He made many trips with the wheelbarrow to fill the trench with stones, using blue clay to bind them together.

The actual building was started with four cornerstones which were checked diagonally. We all watched with excitement as the walls began to go up. The stone walls, two feet thick, were built to a height of seven feet using a line to keep them straight.

The windows were small, but they did let in light during the day. The door was the traditional half door. Since the door faced Trawbreaga Bay and the opening was sheltered from the fierce wind, we were able to keep it open most days to air out the house.

It took over two months for the house to be finished. During the construction people came from the surrounding townlands to check on the progress. Paul went up to the lime quarry and kiln up the hill, in the bog to produce the lime to use in the building of the house. First he quarried the rock. Then he broke the limestone into smaller pieces about the size of an egg. The kiln was a round stone stove built next to the hill. It was about fourteen feet across and about eight feet high. He built a turf fire both underneath and above the lime stone, then left it to burn for a couple of weeks. When it was finished, the white powder was brought down to the building site. It was not only used to make that nice white colour of paint on the walls by adding water, it was also used in-between the rocks as a mortar. It seems that when lime is used, it is easier for the walls to dry out and not hold in the dampness. Crushed limestone is also plowed into some fields when they have not been producing.

I had often noticed a line of damp going up the walls in some houses. When I asked Paddy, he said that they had neglected to lime the walls. I did not understand that because the walls looked white to me. When Paul was building the walls of the new house, I understood, the lime was meant to go in-between the levels of rock in the wall as well.

The plan was to have two floors in the house, two rooms on the ground floor and two rooms on the first floor. The door entered into the kitchen with a door to the upper room off of it. Each room had a separate heat source, a cook-stove in the kitchen and a fireplace in the upper room. The stairwell upstairs was off the kitchen and went up between the rooms in the middle of the house. This new design meant that each room was cosy with the heat, even when the door was opened. No longer would the heat of the fire in the upper room go out the front door every time it was opened. The upper room had a partition on the left side. There was a door in the wall and that small room contained a bed for Paddy and me near the fire. It surrounded a window in the outer wall so that Paddy and I could look out over the street to the fields beyond, toward Slieve Snacht.

The New House built by Mary's son Paul in 1909 when she was 62

It is called the snowy mountain because the snows will lie longer on it than any of the surrounding mountains. There were years when I was a girl that there would be a snow patch still there from the previous winter when it began to snow the next. It was a beautiful vista. Paul took the bedroom upstairs above us and the girls had the other.

There was a big, new cook-stove put into the kitchen. The first time that the girls and I tried to bake a scone, we burnt it so badly that it could have been a door-stopper through the winter. It was so bad that we could not even give it to the chickens. It took some time to learn how to use the new stove, we had been so used to cooking over the open fire with the crane holding the pot. The scones were either over-cooked or doughy in the middle until I learned just how hot to keep the fire.

I still miss my crane over the open fire. The other great feature of the kitchen was the cold water tap that came into the house and brought water into a sink at the back of the kitchen.

Paul had seen this in the homes in Oregon and worked out how to set it up in our new home. Later that next year, when Paul married Mary McCallion from Cabadooey, I had enough experience with the new stove, that I was able to show her how to work the stove as she took over her responsibilities as the woman of the house.

Chapter 29

The Last Weans Leaving
Spring 1911

There was such excitement for the few months leading up to the time that Rosie and Maggie were leaving for Oregon in 1911. Paul had married Mary McCallion from Cabadooey the previous February in 1910 and they were expecting their first wean in the spring of 1911.

Their wedding had lasted a week. It was one of the biggest weddings that anyone had seen for a long time. People came by horse and cart and sidecars to Mary's home place in Cabadooey. There were so many people in sidecars, that they were parked all the way down to the main road, over a mile and a half away.

After the wedding in the chapel, everyone went back to Cabadooey for the wedding breakfast and party. Later the guests went home to milk their cows and tend to their other chores and returned the next night for a party again. The same thing was repeated every night for a week.

That evening, Paul brought Mary home. Rosie was watching at the window for me as I was getting everything prepared. I kept remembering with fondness how welcoming

Nancy had been to me when I was the new bride so many years before. Some of my dear friends had strained relations with their son's wife, and I knew just what to do so that Mary and I continued to get on great.

Rosie said, "Mammy, the newlyweds have arrived."

I dried my hands on my apron, smoothed my hair and went towards the door.

We heard Paul in the street, "You are home now, dear Mary."

We could not make out her reply, but they were both laughing as Paul gallantly swept open the front door and stood back to allow her to cross the threshold first.

She stepped tentatively into the room, a smile still on her face, her eyes adjusting to the dim light of the lantern. She looked right at me, as if to say, what do we do now?

I said, "Ye are welcome home, Mrs. Doherty."

We laughed and embraced.

I said, "Mary, come sit down, here is your chair right next to the stove."

She crossed the floor to the chair.

I turned to my son and said, "Paul, you go out and bring in your wife's things. I have cleared a shelf in the press for her. After a nice cup of tea, she can arrange them where she wants them."

As is customary, it took a little while for us to get used to each other's ways, but we made room for each other and grew to love one another.

After Paul's Mary had settled into the house, the girls, Rosie and Maggie, decided that it was time they went out to Oregon to join the family there, so they began their preparations. Over the next year, we set aside whatever money had been sent home by the others in order to purchase the girls' passage to America.

We realised that neither of the girls had met their sister Kate before. Kate had gone to Oregon in 1888 just after Sadie was born, sponsored by Paddy's sister Kate and her husband,

John Molloy. Our Kate had married James Grant Doherty from Iskaheen when Rosie was three.

James' mother was a first cousin of Paddy's cousin Catherine Doherty Nelson, so since we knew the connection it had not seemed too distant. Kate's eldest girls were just a few years younger than Rosie and Maggie, so they would feel more comfortable with their cousins than their sister who would be like a second mother to them.

It was comforting to me that Kate was so settled. She had 10 children, nine still living, when the girls went out to her. Phil had the four boys and his wife, Margaret McDaid, just discovered that she was increasing again.

Ann's husband, Ed, had returned to Ireland ten years before, just two years after her death to find himself a wife. When he called at the cottage, I do not think that Rosie or Maggie were about, or at least they did not remember meeting him. He married a girl from Malin Head and they lived in Idaho with four or five weans of their own, as well as Annie's daughter, Cassie.

I had hoped that Rosie and Maggie would get a chance to know her, but with Annie gone, there had not been much connection there for many years. Nora had been married to Francis McCabe from Co. Leitrim for a couple of years by then. They already had Elizabeth Mary and Francis Patrick and were expecting that coming summer. Sarah had been in Oregon for a couple of years and the girls were anxious to meet up with her again. They were looking forward to meeting their other relations out in Oregon as well.

With all the emigration over the years, there were more relations and connections in Oregon than in Ireland. The girls were excited to begin their new lives. I remembered that feeling when I thought that I was going to Boston.

I had felt the overshadowing sadness of leaving Paddy behind, but I do remember the excitement and the anticipation of the trip and the new experiences.

The girls were able to take the train to Derry Quay and not make that long walk that I had made those years before. The morning after they had left, I lay there in my bed and realised that for the first time in many years, I only had meself and Paddy to look after. Paul's Mary was so good at keeping house and cooking that I was often just in the way.

That morning, for the first time in my life, I felt that I had no responsibility. And although one might think that it would be wonderful to not have any burdens, in that moment it was sad to me.

I spent the next couple of weeks just wandering around, back and forth, in and out of the cottage, giving the appearance of industry, but not accomplishing anything. I did not have my heart in it.

One day in a rare moment of talking to me about how things were getting on, Paddy looked me in the eye and said, "Well, Mary, ye still have me. We started out just the two of us and it will be grand. Come on, girl, let us get on with it then."

I realised that I did have my life to live, there were things to do, there were people that I could help. Eventually there were the grandchildren. Paul and Mary had nine weans for me to help care for. I especially felt close to Josie, who would sit upon my knee to hear all my stories, but for those weeks back in the spring of 1911, I did feel a little lost.

It was a hard transition for me, no longer having any children of my own to look after and rear. I wondered what I was supposed to be doing to fill my days, but by the time the first letter arrived from Rosie telling us all the news, I was recovered and really enjoyed reading it. It did comfort me to carry her letters around folded up in my sleeve, to read over and over until the next one arrived.

Each of our boys out in Oregon were, of course, running sheep. It was what they knew. It was what they had been taught by their father and he by his father before.

A letter would arrive from Philip to Paddy, telling him how many lambs he had that year, or a story about a particular ewe that worried him, or how to get his dog to work right. Philip would often ask Paddy's advice in the letter and Paddy would insist that I get pen and paper to scribe a response to be sent right back. Paddy would be there eyes closed, with his clay pipe, sitting next to the fire, listening to the letter. It seemed that he could actually see in his mind the whole situation as described by his sons.

Paddy's ability to work with the animals was amazing, especially his dogs. It was a sight to see his dogs work the sheep. From the time a wee pup was born, Paddy would work with him, and train him. Paddy disciplined each pup to the point that by just a set of whistles in a certain pattern, the dog knew to stop or which way to go, to move the sheep, or round them up, even cutting one out from the rest of the flock. Whatever Paddy wanted done, it was as if the dog could read his mind, but really it was the training.

It was a marvelous thing to see, a man and his dog working so well together to care for the sheep. The dogs would be crouched down, out in the field, amongst the sheep, not moving a muscle until instructed by Paddy. With the slightest noise of command, the dog would be up and running, circling this way, or that way, or even running back and forth, stopping, crouching down, creeping forward, stopping again. Whatever the instruction had been, that is what the dog did.

Chapter 30

Rosie's Drawing
1912

osie wrote to us, in one of her first letters home, that it was so bleak and dry in Oregon. She was kept busy with all the nieces and nephews to tend. I am sure that Kate was grateful to have her. I asked Rosie to draw me a picture so that I could better understand what the countryside was like. She had always been such a great scribbler, but she said that she did not have time to draw. There was too much work to be done with Kate already delivered of her eleventh child the previous autumn. Rosie was living in Pendleton working as a housekeeper in one of the big houses there.

When the woman of the house would ask her if she knew how to cook a particular dish, she would nod and say, oh sure, that will be no problem. Then she would go out the back door and down the block to the adjacent houses and ask the other Irish girls how to do whatever it was that she had said she knew how to do.

She would not admit to her employers that she did not know how to prepare what they were asking. She learned how it was to be done. When she had a day off she would take the train to Ione and wait at the livery stable for Phil or James to come in and collect her.

It was such a shame that Rosie would not draw anymore. Paddy and I took great comfort looking at the picture on the wall of our sitting room that she had drawn of the castle by the lake.

Paddy often remarked that he was sure his Rosie would come back home to us but I did not ever believe that.

Rosie's Drawing of Black Rock Castle dated 6 August 1903

I suppose that I was right, because Paddy is now gone and the drawing still sits waiting on the front room wall for Rosie to return.

Looking around the room comforts me. I notice the blackened cast iron cookpot on my own hearth and it reminds me of the continuity of life. There was an element of my mother's hearth brought into my new home when she gave me that steaming pot filled with soup the first morning of my married life. She must have begun making the soup just after getting home from my big day.

That one pot has been with me these long years, a central article in my home. It fed our family through times of plenty and stretched out the staples in the leaner times. It has witnessed the joyful times, the hearty laughter that often filled our home.

It caught a few tears as well, as I stood stirring the soup over the fire in the other moments of my life. In the cold of winter it would heat up the air with the rich steam and in the spring and summer it would strengthen my men for their long labours in the fields. I believe that my life can be measured by the meals from that cookpot. Some were served with love to my family in the fresh breezes of spring or the damp dark nights of the autumn. Other times the meals were served with frustration towards Paddy, the weans or the neighbours, or even with meself.

Chapter 31

Kate Visiting
Summer 1914

I remember the days leading up to the visitors' arrival in the summer of 1914. We had received the letter in the post telling us of their plans. Our Kate and her sister-in-law Mary Doherty Kenny would arrive any day on the ship into Derry Quay. She and Mary would catch the train down from Derry City to Carn and we were to send Paul or someone to meet them at the station house on the Malin Road, to bring their luggage up Ballyloskey. After 26 years away, she was returning home for a visit. When she left us, she was a young, excited 16 year old and now at age 42 she was the mother of twelve herself.

Paddy had wanted Paul to make arrangements to have the house and the wall surrounding the yard painted. Paul decided that he would do it himself, so he bought the paint and set about getting the job done. As what will happen with many big projects, one thing led to another and Paul had not actually put any paint on the brush yet when word came that the ship had been sighted from Malin Head. That meant that the visitors would be arriving up at the house the next day and Paddy was in a huff. He wanted everything to be in order for his Kate to come home.

Paul got word to a couple of the local boys and they painted all through that day, on into the long summers evening and began again in the first morning light. When the job was finished, the white walls shone brightly in the sunshine. The red on the door and window sills was cheery. Mary and I were careful as we brushed the floor and doorstep so as not to get any dirt on the freshly painted walls. In some places it was still a bit wet.

Some of the young ones had gone on to Moville to catch the view of the ship coming down the Foyle. In her last letter Kate wrote with such excitement of her plans. During her visit, she was to take us up on the train to Derry and then onto the Coast Road to the Giant's Causeway.

We had heard it said that the Causeway actually looks like the giant Finn McCool built a road to travel across the water over

The Giants Causeway

172

to Scotland. She wrote us about the brochure she received from the shipping company of the various land tours available.

Paddy was delighted that one of his girls was finally coming back home for a visit. Although he was blind he could recognize people from their voice and the sound of their footfall. Many a time we had tried to trick him, only to have him know exactly who the person actually was.

First, we heard the horse and wagon approaching, then feminine voices raised in excitement and astonishment of the changes that had taken place on the farm. I, of course, ran to the window to catch the first glimpse of our Kate as she descended from the wagon. Peering out into the street, I looked for our Kate and instead saw two grand ladies. Their dresses were of a fashion I had never seen before.

I wondered who these two were as we were expecting our Kate and her sister-in-law. The taller one stood with her back to me as she slowly took off her gloves. As she turned her face to the cottage, I could see that it was our Kate and I gasped.

She walked the few steps to the door, and removed her beautiful hat. Then stooping to come through the door, she saw me and smiled. I returned the smile but then stepped back to give Paddy the first chance to greet our oldest living child. I looked over to him in his chair. He looked as if he was trying to appear relaxed, but knowing him as I did, I noticed him working his lips in wee circles, in that way he did when he was deeply thinking about something.

As the door to the cottage opened and her footfall was heard on the flagstones, Paddy leaned forward, cocking his head, so as not to miss anything.

I heard her whisper, "Oh Da!"

She ran to him, and kneeling before him, laid her head in his lap. Although she was over 40 years of age with grown children of her own, for a moment I saw the little girl hugging her father's knee as he stroked her head to comfort her. No one spoke, time stopped and we felt the bond of family that transcends the years and the miles. I am afraid that I embarrassed meself as I turned my face away to try to stifle the tears. No one seemed to notice, but I think that they knew.

Paddy was not typically a demonstrative man, but he held onto her a bit longer than I would have expected. Finally Kate rose from her knees and looked around the cottage.

Cocking her head to the side as she always did and almost with a sigh, she said, "Oh 'tis grand to be at home again, and look, even though yous are in a brand new house, some things here are not that much changed. The black pot is bubblin' over the fire as it always was and there, there is Mammy's three-legged stool set up close to the fire. Let me just sit here a minute and look at you."

"Mammy where is the basket with your knittin'? Oh, here it is beside me knee, where it should be, next to your stool, where it always has been. Oh 'tis grand to be at home."

She looked around the room.

"I do miss the aul crane over the fire, but your new cook stove is truly wonderful."

She closed her eyes and took in a deep breath.

"And Mammy, I told me husband James as I was leavin' home, that yous would have a hot pot o' tay brewing next to a fresh baked scone when I arrived. It is all so lovely."

We laughed as she went round the room reassuring herself that we were still all the same and for a small moment she was the same young girl that had left home so many years before.

Paddy kept asking, "How does she look, Mary? Tell me how she looks."

Paddy told me later that he knew Kate was well taken care of as he stroked her face and it was not gaunt, and with his hand on her shoulder, he could tell the fine weave to the cloth of her coat. Gripping her hand, he fingered the cuff of her cotton shirt and it was not ragged.

He knew that his children worked hard out in Oregon, but with her visit back home, he then knew first hand, that they were not starving or wearing rags so far away. I could tell by looking at her that she was happy and healthy, but he had to find out for himself in spite of his blindness, that his Kate was doing well and that James was a good husband to her.

He was beginning to accept and feel at peace that his weans had made the right choice to leave home to find a home in Oregon. Before losing his sight he had seen the effects of the impoverished hard life in Ireland on the local beauties in our parish. Womens' health was lost and their fair faces ravaged by harsh conditions and failed crops. We watched as their once lustrous hair became thin and scraggly, their eyes no longer sparkling, the soft bloom of their cheeks now sallow and deep creases surrounded their downturned mouths. He often commented that you could see how hard life was on the faces of the women.

And although he had seen some of the photographs sent back from Oregon over the years, before his sight was taken, it was not until he had Kate by his side that his fear was relieved. It had been difficult for him that all of the weans in turn had left our hearth for America. It was a comfort to him to have her come back, even for such a short visit.

The trip must have been exhausting for them. First they took the Great Northern train from Oregon all the way to the east coast of the States. Kate described the different cars on the train, the famous Pullman sleeper cars with their upper and lower berths, the parlour cars for playing cards and other games and the dining cars. The tables in the dining cars had a short wooden ledge around the edge to keep the dishes and glasses from falling off. The parlour car had an outside viewing platform where they could get a bit of fresh air. Kate mentioned that they felt that they were bouncing up and down for the entire week. It was an exciting adventure as they saw much of the countryside. They then stopped in Boston with my sweet sister Sarah before they caught the ship over the ocean.

I always enjoyed and appreciated the boxes that Sarah would send to us through the years. She was a very thoughtful and generous sister to me and she looked after our Kate well during her visit to Boston. Kate described the great excitement

Sarah and her family had concerning their upcoming trip home later that same summer.

As Kate told us of the total boredom experienced on the ship in addition to the sea sickness and bad weather, I could not ever imagine taking such a trip. Even after enduring all of that, they had the final bit of their trip from Derry down to us. That portion alone of their journey was an excursion that tired me and I always took days to recover.

During Kate's visit that summer she insisted that I travel around with her. I enjoyed the little daytrips out and the beautiful scenery of Ireland that I had never gotten to see before.

I was not able to go with her every day between the work that was for me and the care of Paddy, but I was able to go on quite a few day trips and it was lovely.

In the evening we would rehearse all of our adventures and the vistas we had seen for Paddy as we told him everything we had experienced.

One evening after returning from a trip on the train to Derry City, we were sitting by the fire in the upper room, when Kate remarked, "Sit ye there, Da, I want to show you something."

Paddy said, "What can she show a blind man?"

I responded that perhaps she wanted to share something with him. She quickly left the room and went upstairs to where she had been sleeping. She returned in a few moments with a small package wrapped in brown paper and tied with a string.

"I bought me a souvenir today, Da." She said. "Here let me open the package, and tell me what you think."

It was a wee brown jug, with gold along the top.

"I am planning on setting it on my table each morning when I set out the breakfast. It will remind me of home."

Paddy was full of questions. In which shop had she made the purchase? Had she negotiated a fair price? How would she package it to ensure that it arrived in Oregon safely? He knew the man who owned the shop in Derry and was content that Kate had made a wise purchase.

Paddy had seen some of the countryside himself in his younger years, so sometimes he would interject a question or a comment about a farm or wallsteads that he remembered. As a younger man he had travelled all over Inishowen helping others with clipping their sheep.

The travels around were exciting, but for me my favourite memories of that summer were those of Kate sitting on the small stool next to the fire, her eyes bright telling the stories, with Paddy silently smoking his pipe, nodding his head, both of them smiling, enjoying the time together. He seemed to have more strength that summer when Kate was visiting than he had shown for many years.

Rosie had stayed back in Oregon to mind Kate's children. Originally we had received word that she was coming home as well, but she decided the better of it and remained in Oregon.

Kate told us many times during that visit, that Rosie's decision to stay back in Oregon was a great comfort to her. Kate knew that her family was well cared for. Paddy was still of a mind that she was coming back home soon, although as the days turned into years, I was not convinced that we would ever see our Rosie again.

One afternoon during Kate's visit, Mary Kenny stayed back at the cottage to look after Paddy while Kate and I went out for a walk. She asked if we could take my special walk. I was surprised. I had no idea that the weans even knew about that special walk from my younger days.

She laughed and said, "You would be surprised Mammy. We girls often ask each other out in Oregon, now what would Mammy do or what would Mammy say about that."

That was such a great comfort to me to know that they thought of me over in America.

So down Ballyloskey Road we walked. Crossing the Derry Road, we followed the lane behind the Workhouse, and finally we reached the cool shade around the Glentogher River where it runs into the Donagh River. Dipping our feet in the cool water we rested on my favourite stone. Without speaking we

177

both stood and silently we decided to follow the river, winding through the fields and woods until it emptied into Trawbreaga Bay.

With the wind picking up the ends of her hair and blowing it across her face, she stood like a statue at the shoreline.

Turning her face into the wind, she said, "The wind in Oregon is the one thing that reminds me of home. The weather can be so fierce though, it takes some getting used to. It can be so hot in the summer that it takes your breath away when you come up out of the root cellar and then so bitterly cold in the winter that you canna mind what warmth feels like."

She paused, looking out over the bay at a pair of seagulls dancing in the air above the waves.

Her eyes lit up as she said, "Mammy we have such great craic when everyone ceilis to our home in Blackhorse Canyon. I wish you could see it."

She described the trees that they had planted around their home to give some shade during the summer and protection from the weather in the winter. I could almost see the women sitting in chairs around the yard, with the children running to and fro in the summer sunshine. The men would be off to the side of the yard at the horseshoe pit, challenging each other to a game or head down to the barn to look at a horse.

As she described the ceilis and the other gatherings, I knew that it was a good life that my children had made in America. I was so grateful that the children and their weans kept so close to one another in Oregon, although the distances that they had to travel to see one another seemed daunting to me.

That day was so mild, with barely a breeze, and we sat at the shoreline visiting as mothers and daughters can do. The hours passed by. It was a grand day. I still cherish the memory of that stolen afternoon so long ago.

Paddy and I were grateful to hear first-hand from Kate how each of our family were getting on. We were delighted to hear of their successes and saddened to hear of their struggles.

Wistfully we heard the stories of our many grandchildren as she described their personalities to us.

She was fair, and explained both their talents and weaknesses to us as only a mother and fond aunt could know. We would never know each of them that well. The letters that we had received over the years had given us the news but through Kate's stories we were comforted with the knowledge that our family was coping the best they could with their life experiences.

My sister Sarah did come to visit later that same summer. She brought her children and a couple of their cousins back home

Mary's sister Sarah (standing, fourth from the left) and her family onboard the ship in 1914

for a month's visit. They sailed from New York City to Ireland on the *Maurentonia*. It was wonderful to finally meet my nephew and nieces after reading about them for years in the letters that Sarah sent home. We had much excitement in our wee townland that year with all the visitors.

The first morning after Sarah and her family arrived, the boys went up the hill with Paul to help bring in the turf. Paul willingly took all of the visitors who wanted to help up with him. They were a fine looking group heading out in the morning with their white shirts shining, their trousers creased and their boots polished. The day was a lovely summer day with just a bit of a breeze. Paul's Mary took me up with her in the wagon a few hours later when she took the dinner out to them.

The group that I saw standing wearily in the bog fields did not look anything like the same young men who had practically run up the road heading for their adventure. With the sweat pouring down their dirty faces and dripping onto their wrinkled and bog stained shirts, they eagerly sat down on the rocks by the road to eat the repast.

I noticed the red splotches on their arms and faces with the welts beginning to rise and asked Paul what had happened. He laughed and reminded me that the midgies and the biting flies love visitors. When I got back to the house that evening, I boiled some carrageen moss to make a salve for the welts. Even with the salve, those bites were inflamed and sore for a couple of weeks after that first day, and no one would take Paul up on his offer to join him in the bog again. We all laughed for days at the treatment that the visitors received from the local midgies and biting flies.

It was common in every house for the young ones to leave home. They left seeking a better, more prosperous life. They worked hard, married, reared their own families, sending money periodically to support and sustain their parents, but they never returned home. That story of heartache and loss ran through our history for centuries. It is Ireland's story. However, when relations began returning home for short visits, we recognized that the separation was not necessarily permanent. There began to be hope that families could be reunited.

Later that Autumn, after many months of visiting and travelling about the country, the holiday makers were to return to America. Our Paul organised a party in our house for the night before they all were leaving on the boat. As I have said, it is our tradition to have a big send off for those who are leaving. When Kate left the first time at age 16, the party was called an American Wake. Now we call it a "Big Night". Friends and relations gathered at the house in the early evening after chores were done. After a while one of the McLaughlins from down the road picked up his fiddle and started the dancing.

Songs were called for; each person had their party piece prepared. Some songs speak of epic love, others recall great loss. We sing songs of emigration, some are hopeful, others forlorn. There are songs of battles won and battles lost. These are the songs of our life and our land, our heritage. Long ago Shanachies, the clan historians, would sing the songs for their clan; now we carry that tradition forward as we sing the old songs.

Amidst all the frivolity, I recognized an underlying melancholy that we all tried to ignore. Our Kate was leaving again. Although it was with great joy we had welcomed her arrival, it was with equal sadness that we said goodbye. Through that last night, our eyes would meet across the room and somehow we both knew that we would never see each other again. The ache was palpable underneath the excitement of the party.

In spite of the upcoming loss, it was great craic altogether; the laughter, the singing, the dancing, the drink. Suddenly, it seemed that dawn was upon us.

I heard someone say, "Again the night has flown, and we greet the dawn at a ceili up at Paul's." I laughed to meself as I thought of the reputation we were getting amongst the neighbours.

I realised that Paul himself had not sung yet, just as I heard our Kate say, "Now Paul, it would be hard going to leave

Ballyloskey again, without hearing from you now. Ye would not be asking me do that, now would ye?"

He laughed whilst clearing his throat and asked, "Kate, now what song would that be that ye have a mind to hear?"

Kate shook her finger toward him, and said, "Ye have only one song that ye even know dear brother, so sit yourself right down and get on with it."

"Ye only had to ask me sister. Ye only had to ask."

He then began his party piece, with a voice so rich and low. Everyone stopped talking to hear the beautiful ballad that Paul always sang at every party.

I am always light-hearted and easy,
Not a care in the world have I,
For I know I am loved by a colleen
And I could not forget if I tried.
She lives far away o'er the mountain
Where the little birds sing on the trees;
In a cottage all covered with ivy
My Eileen is waiting for me.
It's over, it's over the mountain
Where the little birds sing on the trees,
In a cottage all covered with ivy
My Eileen is waiting for me.

The time I bade good-bye to Eileen
Is a time I will never forget
For the tears bubbled up from their slumbers
I fancy I see them yet;
They looked like the pearls in the ocean
As she wept her tale of love.
And she said "My dear boy, don't forget me
Till we meet here again or above."
It's over, it's over the mountain
Where the little birds sing on the trees,
In a cottage all covered with ivy
My Eileen is waiting for me.

We all had heard Paul sing his song "Where my Eileen is Waiting for Me" many times before, yet that morning as the sun was beginning to light the eastern sky it was particularly poignant as we thought of all of our loved ones who were no longer with us. After Paul's song finished, the party was over. Someone said that we were all too melancholy to continue. I think that we were all just tired. It was morning after all.

Travelling back to America on the ship together with our Kate and Mary Kenny, were Annie McCabe, our Nora's sister-in-law from Leitrim, and William and Susie Ruddy from Glentogher. Kate told us that the journey back to America was much more lively than the trip home to Ireland. Susie had already been out to America and she had returned home that summer to collect her brother William.

The Ruddys are shirt-tail relatives of Paddy's. They are William Callahan's grandchildren from his first wife, who died. Their mother, Mary Ann Callahan Doherty, had left Ireland years before, after her first husband, William Ruddy died. She believed that her poverty was causing her children to starve. She left her children in her step-mother's care in Glentogher and went to Boston to work in a bakery and began to send money home. From Boston she travelled to Morrow County, Oregon to live with her half sister Katie Doherty on a ranch in Sand Hollow. Mary Ann took her spinning wheel from home here, out to Boston and then around the Horn all the way to Oregon. Out there she married Philip Hirrell and they had four of a family. Mary Ann and Phillip had been childhood friends here in Carn. Now Susie was taking William out to America to meet his brothers and sisters and finally live with his mother.

Kate and the group all travelled together on the *Pannonia*. The ship is part of the Anchor Line fleet. They sailed away from Derry City on 3rd October and arrived after ten days journey at Ellis Island in the harbor of New York City. Sarah and her family had left us on the 13th of September on the SS *Cameronia*. Their crossing was only nine days to arrive at Ellis Island on the 21st of September. It was with great humour that we discussed the Boston connections travelling quicker than the Oregon connections back to America.

Kate later wrote to us that there were about 200 people on their ship. Fresh water was in short supply during the journey and nine passengers were detained at Ellis Island for health inspections. Most of the passengers were Irish or Scots, but Kate mentioned that there was a group of nine who were Russians emigrating from Lithuania. They did not speak much English, so the only thing that the other passengers knew was that they were going to family in Pennsylvania.

When Kate returned to her home in Oregon that October, it was as if she took the brightness of the summer's sun with her. Paddy seemed very sad for weeks after her departure.

My attention, however, was turned to Paul's Mary. She was increasing and the baby was expected before Christmas. Their two boys, Packie (age three and a half) and Neilly (age two), were hoping for another brother. Although they were momentarily disappointed by the arrival of a baby sister, all the rest of us were delighted when our wee Josie made her appearance the end of November. A new wean brings hope to a house and that is surely what happened in our house in 1914.

Chapter 32

Nora Drowned In July
1 September 1916

O n September the first, 1916 an envelope arrived from Kate in Oregon. Shrouded in black, I knew that it was not good news, so I could not open it. The black border on the envelope tells the story even if you do not know who is dead. A message of death of a loved one is never welcome news.

A black border envelope used to announce a death in the family

The letter was months old, so I decided that the news could wait until Paddy and Paul returned home. I left it in the middle of the kitchen table, and every time I passed it that day, I would avert my eyes. It probably was more bothersome to avoid knowing what had happened than it would have been to just read the letter and learn the truth.

Finally, hours later, the men returned home from the fields. Paul was the first through the door. He saw the letter and looked at me.

No words were spoken but his eyes said, "Well, would yous like me to open it?"

Closing my eyes, I slowly nodded. I could not bear even to touch it. I led Paddy to his chair by the fire, while Paul picked up the letter. He sat down, sighed and with resolve, opened the envelope.

It was our dear Nora, God rest her. She and her son Philip had died in a tragic flash flood on 1 July, two months ago to the day. Letters took so long to come from America.

Just days before receiving the black edged envelope, I had been thinking about Nora and her family. I thought that she should have given birth to the new baby by then and would be preparing to mark little Philip's third birthday later in the month. My mind had thought about them the whole day long.

Upon receiving the letter, I realised that instead of joy those past months, their life was full of grieving, the three small children wondering what had happened to their Mum and baby brother, and poor Frank, wondering how he was going to get along without his Nora. I thought that after two months, they would be well into their grieving, but for Paddy and me, that day was just the start. The letter said that they had sent a wire a few days after the accident, but we never received it.

As I sat there in shock, I remembered that day, the beginning of July, when I had heard the howling of the banshee. If you have never heard it, I can only describe it as a thin, screeching sound somewhere between the wail of a woman and the moan of an owl. It is unquestionably from the other world. Immediately after the sound ceased, I had a terrible sense of tragic premonition concerning Nora. I went to find Paddy to tell him what I had experienced. We waited for news.

It turned out that my experience was on the very day of the flood. But when we did not receive any word, Paddy said that the worrying was unfounded. Now my worst fears were confirmed. Learning the truth of our great loss closer to the actual time might have been easier to handle, but we will never know.

Oh me Nora, sweet, tender, gentle Nora. Even after all these years, I still canna believe that she is gone.

There had been a flash flood, similar to what happened to Nora, in Heppner just two years after she went out to Oregon. June 1903 saw the normally placid Willow Creek burst its banks during an intense rain and hail storm. The city of Heppner, at the foothills of the Blue Mountains in eastern Oregon, was almost completely destroyed, many buildings were leveled and some were moved from their foundations and had to be torn down. Two hundred twenty of Heppner's 1,400 residents died in the flood.

The letters that we received from our girls at that time were so descriptive that I could just see the bodies lining the main street with all the buildings in shambles behind. The Heppner Flood was only 13 years prior and that disaster was still fresh in the minds of all the residents of the county.

Paddy wondered how Nora and the baby could have gotten caught in the flood. Kate's letter explained that three smaller canyons converge on McDonald Canyon above where Frank and Nora's homestead was. It was a dry day that day and the flood was completely unexpected. A heavy cloudburst had hit up in the mountains and a wall of water 15 feet high was roaring down the canyon. One of the ranch hands had heard the approach of the deluge and ran to the house with two other hands to warn the family. Frank was in Heppner attending a funeral. Nora sent the three men ahead with the children. She was last out of the house, carrying little Philip. She had taken a few moments to retrieve the household savings, her pin money.

Bessie told the story of reaching the wooden walk that led out of the house and went up the hill. As she felt the walk begin to give way in the water she looked back to see her mother mouthing the words urging her and her brother and sister to hurry toward the Hirl homestead.

Paddy's sister Rose and her husband Edward were their nearest neighbour. They lived on higher ground a few miles away. Bessie grabbed a fence post and struggled to follow the ranch hands, one of whom was carrying Mary. The man carrying Mary also reported on being saved from the rushing water by holding onto a fence, as he and the others led the children out of the canyon.

When the wall of water hit, Nora, pregnant and carrying the little boy, had no chance of escaping. Her skirt quickly became waterlogged by the flood waters and she fell. No one could rescue her and Philip before the water carried them away. When the children reached the Hirl ranch house, they were taken in by the family.

Later that same week we received a letter from Paddy's sister Rose. She wrote that she knew Nora was gone as soon as she saw the three children trudging mournfully alone without their mother. She knew that Nora was pregnant and must have had small Philip with her. Rose told us that when Frank returned home to find the ravages of the flood, he was devastated. The next day, he and others searched down the canyon, following the route of the wall of water that had hit the house.

The search party found Nora five miles down the canyon, the battering of the water having ripped off her clothes. One of the men threw a coat over Nora. They searched on for Philip and found him later. Nora and Philip were buried in the same grave together in the Heppner Cemetery.

The letters that we received from Oregon over the years would contain word about Nora's children. They had been sheltered as much as possible from the details of the tragedy.

They were not told of the death of their mother and brother for two weeks. Every day, they waited for her return, hoping she would recover from the shock of being knocked down by the water. They resolutely believed that she was alive and would return to them.

As with many children who lost one parent or another, the relatives stepped in to look after them, but they missed their mother dreadfully.

Although the original house was still standing after the flood, the damage to the lower floor was so severe that Frank had the house torn down. The new house was set up on the hillside, above the cottonwoods that still sheltered the canyon where the original homestead dwelling was built.

Anne McCabe, Frank's sister from Leitrim, was sent for and moved in to keep house for Frank and the children. She is the same young Anne McCabe who travelled back with our Kate when she returned home to Oregon in 1914. Later, when their aunt Anne had married, Bessie and Frank stayed with their dad but Mary lived for a time with her aunt, our Rosie. Rose and her husband Bill looked after two nieces for a time, Mary McCabe and Mae Doherty, both of the girls having lost their mothers at a very tender age.

Nora was considered one of the most beautiful women in Morrow County, and she also was warm, loving, and full of fun. She and Frank made a handsome couple when they were married, but the death of his wife left Frank a lonely man with a harsh view of the world.

That evening reading the letter from Kate, I could tell that Paddy was devastated. I wished that we would have turned to one another in those difficult moments of grief. We could have helped each other through the trials of life that come to everyone, and yet we were silent, barely able to look each other in the eye.

It was over a week before Paddy could even speak about the mundane parts of our life. He never did speak her name again. He just carried that grief in his heart, uncomforted, to the end of his days.

189

Chapter 33

Women Suffragettes
1918

There was such excitement in our local area. Everyone was talking about it. Huge gatherings called rallies were being organised and held around the country. These women, suffragettes they called themselves, were fighting for the rights of women. They said that we should be able to vote, to own property ourselves, and to be elected to office in the government.

Without these things, the suffragette women did not believe that they are being treated as equal to men. I have wondered what caused these women to believe that men and women should be treated the same.

I thought back on my life, and maybe it is not typical of all women, but I have worked alongside Paddy on our farm, and shared experiences dealing with our neighbours. We all discussed the local politics and even the gossip repeated across the ditches.

I was personally responsible for feeding, clothing, and training the children, deciding what repairs were needed to be done first on the house and what could wait. I decided which crops to plant in the kitchen garden, when to harvest the sally garden, and when we needed more turf. Those things were of great importance in our lives. I often said to my sister in law Maggie that with all these decisions that we women had to make, surely the men could at least be responsible for the voting.

I did go to one of the suffragette rallies. Paddy was not sure that it was worth my time, but that was all he said about it. The speakers were very well prepared and caused great emotional responses in the crowd. It was easy to get swept away by their speeches. But the stories that they kept telling were not what I had experienced in life.

I know some women in our townland who were not treated well by their husbands. But that was not the case with me. I knew even that day at the rally that the women would be given the vote and the other rights they wanted. It did not change my life much, but it did open the door for my daughter and granddaughters.

These ideas are not new. They have their roots in the ancient Brehon laws that governed Ireland prior to the English occupation of our land. Women were the equal of men, and could vote, own property and even govern when called upon.

My girls in Oregon were facing the same thing out there. They had rallies and marches across America. In America, at first women were allowed to vote in the local school elections and then eventually they were given the vote for the national elections. It seems that the position of women from my generation to my daughters' expanded past the traditional role of home and children to turn their faces to events outside their own hearth.

I fear that the children will not be looked after as these new ideas change our society.

Chapter 34

Our Fiftieth Anniversary
Thursday, 15 May 1919

I was looking at the photograph of our fiftieth wedding anniversary and I thought back to those times so long ago. I often wondered, although I never asked him, why he waited so long to ask me to marry him. I had always felt that we were supposed to be together.

There were not many surprises over the 50 years that we were married. I knew that he was ornery and I knew that he was stubborn, but I also knew that he could laugh and I knew his sense of humour. The good times that we had in life laughing together got us through some pretty difficult trials.

The anniversary had been a glorious day: not only was the weather incredible, which you can never rely on in May, but the gathering of friends and relations was memorable. The generous spread of food prepared by the younger women was beautiful to behold. The gentle sounds of laughter and banter drifted along with the light breeze. I sat at the end of the garden and beheld the activity around me. Paddy sat in his chair with a soft smile on his face. Someone, our Paul probably, had put an empty chair next to him. Each person coming up to greet him would announce themselves as they sat down. Some would yell their name a little loudly.

He would chastise them and say, "Be a bit quieter man, I am blind, not 'def'."

He knew most people by the sound of their walk or their voice. It amazed me how he could recognize others. He still was sharp and would remember what he had been told the week or month before. Who had planted what crop in which field, who had trouble with the lambing or a particular new farming idea.

The younger men liked to sit and have a chat with Paddy. Both men would benefit. Paddy could talk knowledgably about the European markets and the impact of the Great War on the local farmers. It would often surprise the other men. They did not know that I read the paper to him after Paul was finished with it, cover to cover.

Mary and Paddy's 50th wedding anniversary picture, Ballyloskey 1919

He really enjoyed the anniversary.

I remember saying to him as we were ending the day, "Would not it have been great if the Newmans had come up to the party? They are relations after all."

He turned to me with his sightless eyes, and I could see on his face that he was still not going to talk to me about whatever had happened between himself and his cousin Yankee Pat Newman.

I remember that there had been a bit of tension between the two houses of the Newman's when we were first married, but everyone at least was talking to one another. I do not know exactly the full story, but I mind Paddy coming home one evening for tea, just furious.

He kept muttering over and over, "That ewe is mine."

Finally, I said, "What are ye on about"?

He told me that one of his ewes had gone missing and he saw it in Wee Paddy Newman's field. (He was still called Wee Paddy then. His name did not change to Yankee Pat until he had come back from America.)

Both Paddys believed that the ewe was his own.

My Paddy said to me, "I know the face of that ewe as well as I know your own, Mary dear. That ewe is mine, but that eegit insists that she is his."

I never again heard a word about it, but I wonder if that was the start of all the trouble between the two families. Both men were pleasant to one another after that for years, just nodding in hello as we passed by on a Sunday.

After time went on it seemed that bitterness crept in the middle and they began to look the other way when they would pass one another on the street. You cannot keep things like that from the children and often they will take the attitudes one step further without even knowing or understanding the causes.

It seems so sad when relations fall out. Did it really start between Big Paddy and Wee Paddy? I sometimes wondered if maybe the seeds of this came from the generation before. Did the two Newman brothers, Philip and Jimmy, get along? Or did they have jealousy and rivalry? It is often hard to tell. Even if people are reared in the same house, they may not be friends as adults.

Chapter 35

Independence
1920 and 1921

At the time of the Black and Tans, the "Pauls" house was a safe-house. The Black and Tans were members of the Royal Irish Constabulary Reserve Force and were paid the relatively good wage of 10 shillings a day plus full board and lodging. This police force was organised in an extraordinary fashion. British ex-servicemen were recruited by the British authorities in 1920 for their recent experience with weapons and warfare. The Black and Tans official functions were to be as sentries, guards, escorts for government agents, and crowd control. But they became infamous for terrorizing the Irish Catholics.

During that time, the Irish Republican Army men used to arrive at night on bicycles. Because they were on the run, they were tired and hungry; they would have to be fed and given a bed for the night.

Paul would have to carry the bicycles, one at a time, over to the road at the bottom of Layard's land, to the place that they knew behind a certain ditch and hide the bicycles there. After the

IRA men had been fed and had a sleep they would take off then over the fields and collect their bicycles.

I would get cross about this because we would make our bread for the day, and when these men would arrive unannounced and unplanned for in the middle of the night, they had to be given the food. We had no choice but to feed them even though it meant that we would be short of bread in our house in the morning, while the IRA men were fed. On those days we had to resort to porridge for breakfast. It was not usually meant for breakfast. I could also choose to get up early and make another scone, but this made me cross as well.

The mainstay of our daily food was home baked bread (also called a scone), spuds and porridge. We would drink the buttermilk from the churn after making the butter. We had fish on Fridays and sometimes a bit of meat on a Sunday.

Not everyone in the townland could afford the meat, but we were blessed to be able to eat a chicken every so often. Sometimes we would have eggs if there was a surplus, but we would usually be better off selling the eggs rather than eating them.

Even after the shirt factory on Bridge Street came to Carn, many women were able to squirrel away some pin money selling eggs to the grocer. The grocer man came to the house once a week, his old horse pulling his cart laden with everything imaginable that a woman could want to run a home.

Every week I would buy a sack of flour, some baking soda, porridge oats, tea, sugar, salt and soap. Some days I would have enough money just to buy what we needed, so I would sell the eggs. Other times I would barter the eggs for some of the order. The used flour sacks, cleaned, sewn together and stuffed with feathers would make a nice new bed.

There was always talk in every house about going to America. Some folks said that it was worse after the famine, that many people had just given up hope. There seemed to be no chance for a young person to have a bit of land, create a home and raise a family in this place that we all loved so much.

So people would leave. We would all talk of their leaving for months ahead. Big parties were planned in the days before their scheduled departure. It was as if they were being waked, as if they were going to die. Really they were dead to us, because we never had an expectation of seeing anyone again once they left for America.

This emigration would always anger Paddy. Even from the time of my earliest memories, others would talk of the opportunities the ones that were leaving would have in America. But Paddy would remark that they were breaking the hearts of their mothers and fathers and grannies and grandas. He could never understand why they would leave.

He would ask them on the night of the parties, "How could you leave this land? How can you leave your home? How could you leave your family? How could you do it"?

He never did find understanding.

I think that is why it broke a bit more of his heart each time one of our children would start out for America, in those earlier years. And even when the last of the weans were gone, he pined for them, wondering over and over how could they leave. It broke his heart.

But I do mind Paddy and my brother Hugh sitting down in front of the house, one early spring evening, discussing the most recent ones who had left on the road to Derry. They had to leave in the spring time so that the crossing on the ships would be easier and swifter.

Then they would arrive in Boston or New York or Halifax in time to make preparations for the coming winter. So the ships would leave in April and May or June. It was always a sad time.

The spring planting finished on their parents' farms, the young ones would leave, hoping that the old ones would be taken care of by the relations or by the neighbours. The harvest in the autumn would be bittersweet with thoughts of the ones who went away always on the mind.

Chapter 36

A Letter from Rosie
1924

osie was such a great letter writer. She wrote letters to me and letters to Sarah or Paul's Mary. She even wrote letters to Paul's children. Even though none of Paul's weans ever met Rosie, they all felt as though they knew her through the letters that came from Oregon. Josie especially would wait for the letters to arrive.

About two months after we had written one, she would wait by the window looking over the road for the mail cart to lumber up Ballyloskey. Mickey the Post would always wave to her, even if he was not stopping. It was far more exciting for the children to have him pull into the street, hitch his horse to the post and stop in for a cup of tea and a chat while delivering a letter or a package.

Rosie's letters always seem to be full of interesting stories and information. She had a way of describing a party or an event that made you feel as if you were sitting in the corner of the room watching everything. Even without a picture, we knew what it looked like out in Oregon.

She would describe what everyone was doing, what their plans were, what had worked out and what was still hoped for. It made the distance not seem so far. We knew all the stories, who had come out, who had gone home, who had gotten married, who had given birth and who, unfortunately, had died. It helped me to feel as if I were a part of my girls' lives.

Rosie described the ceilis at the different houses. How they all would pull the wagons into the fields, near the house. The children would be bedded down with quilts in the back of the wagons while their parents danced the old dances and sang the old songs through the night. The weans were safe enough out under the Oregon stars overnight as there was never any rain in the summer and hardly any rain in the winter either.

The weather there was very hot in the summer and cold in the winter. She described the dust that would blow into the house whenever a door or a window was opened. She was forever brushing the floor to get out the dust. Rosie would often write to us that the wind reminded her of home.

Maggie did not write as often at first after getting to Oregon and then later it was only at Christmas. Margaret, as she began to call herself, had found love while visiting relations in Portland. She and her husband moved to a place called Renton in Washington state. Her husband Michael Creegan, originally from Leitrim, was an insurance salesman and Maggie seemed to be getting on well. She had a lovely home and eventually had seven children. She sent me a photograph or two over the years.

All of them looked beautiful and brilliant. Margaret seemed to be well pleased with her life and quite delighted with how things turned out. She did not keep in close contact with Kate or Rosie, but she was happy and I was glad for her and the life that she had made. I had read many letters over the years from our family in Oregon, some of them held great news and others great sadness.

I do mind one letter from our Rosie in the summer of 1924. It was a little late in coming but was particularly pleasing to read. That morning I peered through the glass to see nine year old Josie bounding up the lane and into the street beside the cottage.

"Granny, Granny a letter has come from America to Aunty Sarah. She says we are all to come tonight after tea to hear the letter from Rosie, we are going, are we not?"

Rosie had written at last. We had been awaiting the news of her big day since her wedding in February.

It was only fitting that Rosie would write to Sarah. The two of them had always been close. It was a hard choice for our Sarah when she decided to leave Oregon and return home the previous year. I was delighted to have her home, but sometimes there was a wistful look in her eye and I knew that she missed her sister.

Her own wedding the previous June had been a special day for me. With the seven girls born to me, I never dreamed as I was rearing them, that I would only be at one wedding as the bride's mother.

It was when I was helping Sarah with her preparations, either sewing her clothes, or gathering her household things, such as her churn, her dishes and bedclothes, that I would wistfully think of the others already married. I had missed out on helping them prepare for their marriages. I was grateful for those who had helped each of them get ready for their own houses out in Oregon. It was so far away.

That night we went to Sarah's after the chores were done to hear the letter read. We sat around her fire as she took out her reading glasses and opened the letter. I sat there with my eyes closed so that I could better imagine each detail that Rosie was describing.

She wrote that her husband Bill Doherty is a tall man. She thinks that he is handsome. We all laugh. Paddy said that he hoped Rosie found her husband handsome, as she was going to have to look at him across the table for a very long time. Rosie says that he does not talk much, but he can laugh at himself and at life. We have found through the years that laughter can help.

203

Bill has built her a nice house with a fence around it in a place called Juniper Canyon. There is a covered porch at the front and at the back. There are three rooms downstairs: one is the kitchen, one is the wash room, and one is the sitting room. The staircase runs up the middle of the house. There are two bedrooms up the stairs. One is half way up on the left and the other at the top on the right.

It sounded like she was far away from everyone, but she said that all the farms were far apart there. She and Bill have about a thousand acres, they run sheep and do some wheat farming. We could not imagine such a large amount of land to care for. Bill is in the sheep business with his brothers, and it seems like they are hard working boys.

She planted some more trees around the house as is customary there. It makes a break from the wind and provides some shade in the summer. She always had admired the flowers and shrubs in others' gardens. I wondered if she would be able to have flowers in that dry country.

Paddy's niece Ellen "Callahan", who is married to Edward McDaid of Glenkeen, told Rosie about her own first year in Oregon, back in 1898. Ellen was so tired of not seeing green anywhere in the countryside, that one day she was shocked when she spotted a bit of green a long way off at the top of the hill behind the house. She was so desperate for home that she ran to the spot, thinking all the while that it would be a nice flower or something beautiful, only to find a bitter weed.

It was green all right, but it was just a bit of cheat grass growing there. She said that she sat right down on the ground and had a good cry. Drying her tears, she returned to the house determined to make the best of it and not willing to let the others know of her sadness.

Rosie said that in the spring the hills did remind her of Donegal. The spring rains bring the new growth of the crops and grass and that would make the hills green for a month or so. But by summer they were brown and dusty.

Rosie said that the dust can choke your throat if you are not careful to wear a handkerchief across your mouth and nose. She wrote that she is forever brushing the floor and never can get the dust off of it. As soon as she opens a door or a window to cool the house, the wind gushes in and the floor is covered in sand again.

Most of their fields have sand in them. It is odd that this Newman family cannot seem to escape having their fields afflicted with sand, either in the sand dunes of Ireland or in the sand dune hills of Oregon. The family was given the Newman nickname when they moved up to Ballyloskey from the Isle of Doagh around 1785. On the Isle, their fields had been eroding from the sea over many years and were finally covered in sand. In Ballyloskey, they were the new men Dohertys that leased the fields at the top of the brae.

The wind blows the same in Morrow County as it does in Carn, so they are all well used to it, but the terrible heat and the dust take some getting used to. Rosie mentioned that it is a torture to cook over the wood cook-stove during the heat of the summer.

With the sweat dripping off her, yet not cooling her a bit, she has to make meals for not only her husband, but also the ranch hands and others helping with the planting first and later with the harvesting. She would labour all morning to get the food out for the men at midday when they came in from the fields. She wrote that she tries to set the food out in the shade of the trees so that they can have a short break from the heat of the sun.

She has planted and is tending some grass around her house, so that she has a bit of green to brighten her day when she looks out the window. Even though the rest of the view is brown, she said that it makes her feel closer to home when she can kick off her shoes and walk in the cool green grass just outside her own door.

The letter was finished too quickly and Sarah folded it up and placed it on the top shelf of the kitchen dresser so we could take it down often and re-read Rosie's news. I dreamt that night of a sandy brown place with no flowers and hoped that my girls were happy.

Mary in about 1923

Chapter 37

My Final Comments
26 March 1932

have finally finished telling the story of my life. It has taken me the better part of three years to write this book. I think that I have been able to keep it a secret from the family, although I think that Josie has her suspicions about what I have been writing in my wee notebooks that I have collected from the newsagents.

Over the past few days, I have read what I wrote through from start to finish. I was thinking that I would check for mistakes or omissions, but instead of correcting anything, I really enjoyed reliving the experiences. I laughed and I cried as I remembered each story and person in turn.

For the most part, I lived my life day in and day out filled with the common labours of rural Ireland. Politics or the world stage was never anything that I paid much attention to although the actions of the great men and women of the world did impact the course of my life in Ballyloskey.

Daniel O'Connell, the great liberator, died the year I was born. The law repealing the payment of mandatory tithes to the established church was passed the year Paddy and I married. The Great War was raging across the world the year that I buried my Paddy and yet I took almost no notice of these major world events. My life was filled with events concerning my family and friends.

I wonder what the children will think when they find my manuscript. I hope that they will realise the great adventure I had in life. I also hope that they will appreciate the strong legacy that I have wanted to pass on down to them.

I never did make any corrections to this book as I read it through to the end. It stands as I wrote it.

Tonight as I write these last sentences, I am so very tired. I think that I will just head to bed tonight and perhaps I will start through my book again in the morning after my rest.

Epilogue

Granny Mary Hudie died that night after her last entry.

When she did not arise in the early morning of Sunday the 27th of March, as was her custom, Josie looked into her Granny's bedroom only to discover that Granny Mary was already gone.

The house was full for the wake and her funeral mass filled the chapel. She was well buried.

Josie found this manuscript when she took Granny Mary's knitting basket to sit beside her own bed a few weeks later.

Granny Mary Hudie did leave us a strong legacy, and she will be long remembered. We hope that you have enjoyed her story.

Mary Doherty's family

Bibliography

A Walk through Doagh Famine Village. (2009). Pat & Martina Doherty.

Beattie, S. (2004). *Donegal*. England: J.H. Haynes & Co.

Bonner, B. (1991). *Our Inis Eoghain Heritage*. Limerick, Ireland: Pallas Publication Ltds.

Bonner, B. (1995). *Derry an Outline History of the Diocese*. Limerick: Pallas Publication Ltds.

Canning, B. (2007). *Bishop John Keys O'Doherty of Derry 1889-1907*. Ireland: Limavady Printing Company Ltd.

Colhoun, M. (1995). *The Heritage of Inishowen*. Dublin, Ireland: Impact Printing of Coleraine Ltd.

Danaher, K. (1985). *The Hearth and Stool and All! Irish Rural Households*. Dublin, Ireland: The Mercier Press Limited.

Delaney, Mary. (1973). *Of Irish Ways*. United States of America: Dillon Press.

Dorian, H. (2000). *The Outer Edge of Ulster*. Dublin, Ireland: The Lilliput Press Ltd.

Doyle, J. (1854). *Tours in Ulster*. Dublin, Ireland: Davidson Books.

Drinkwater, C. (2001). *The Hunger*. United Kingdom: Scholastic Children's Books.

Durnin, P. (2005). *Tillies*. Guildhall Press.

Evans, E. (1942). *Irish Heritage*. Dundalk, Ireland: Dundalgan Press.

Evans, E. (1957). *Irish Folk Ways*. Boston, Mass: Routledge & Kegan Paul Ltd.

Grimes, M. (2008). *Till We Meet Again*. Co. Tyrone: Cregg Publishing.

Hasson, G. (1997). *Thunder & Clatter*. L' Derry, Northern Ireland: Guild Hall Press.

Hoad, J. (1987). *This is Donegal Tweed*. Donegal Republic of Ireland: Shoestring Publications.

Lockington, W.J. (1920). *The Soul of Ireland*. London: Harding & More, Ltd.

MacLaughlin, J. (2007). *Donegal the Making of a Northern County*. Dublin, Ireland: Four Courts Press.

Maghtochair, (1985). *Inishowen: It's History, Traditions, and Antiquities*. Dublin, Ireland: Three Candles Printers Ltd.

Manning, A. (2003). *Donegal Poitin*. Somewhere in Donegal: Donegal Printing Company.

McCarroll, S. & Harkin, M. (1984). *Carndonagh*. Republic of Ireland: Cahill Printers Limited.

McCool, S. (2003). *A Donegal Twilight*. Donegal, Ireland: Browne Printer Ltd.

McMahon, S. (1995). *The Homes of Donegal*. Dublin, Ireland: Mercier Press.

McLaughlin, J. (2001). *Carrowmenagh, History of a Donegal Village and Townland*. Dublin, Ireland: JAML.

O'Brien, J. (1953). *The Vanishing Irish*. New York: McGraw Hill.

O'Grady, P. *Donegal in Song and Story*. Dublin, Ireland.

O'Regan, P. (1997). *Healing Herbs in Ireland*. Dublin, Ireland: Primrose Press.

O'Sullivan, J. *Breaking Ground, The Story of William T. Mulvany*. Cork, Ireland: Mercier Press.

Sharkey, O. (1985). *Ways of Old Traditional Life in Ireland* . Dublin, Ireland: The O'Brien Press Ltd.

Shaw-Smith, D. (1984). *Ireland's Traditional Crafts*. London: Thames and Hudson Ltd.

Taylor, A. (1988). *To School Through the Fields*. New York, NY: St. Martins Press.

Whyte, R. (1994). *1847 Famine Ship Diary the Journey of an Irish Coffin Ship*. Cork, Ireland: Mercier Press.

tradítional írish herbal medicinal remedies

Bilberry (Whin berries)   These berries are called fraochán in Irish, traditionally gathered the last Sunday in July called Fraughan Sunday. The berries grow in pairs on the bush. They improve eyesight, used for the treatment of night vision and to stop macular degeneration. The leaves will lower blood sugar, but also inhibit liver function, so long term use of the leaves is not recommended.

Blackberry   The roots of this bramble are used as a decoction for treating diarrhea in children. The roots, leaves and berries can be used as an astringent. The sap can be effective for promoting hair growth. A vinegar made from this plant can be useful for fevers and colds. It also will rid the system of deposits of gout and arthritis.

Buttercup   Also called crowfeet – make an ointment with the petals or with bruised leaves and mix with mustard. It is good to use on blisters. It is not to be taken internally as it has an unpleasant taste and will cause blisters on the tongue.

Chamomile   This plant was used to cure consumption and pleurisy. It is a relaxant and helps to reduce pain. It can ease vomiting in the early months of pregnancy and can help with menopausal problems, painful periods or lack of periods. It is useful in the

213

treatment of diarrhea, colicky pains, gastritis, stomach spasms and nervous indigestion. It is used to dissolve gallstones. It is believed by some to prevent nightmares in children if taken before going to bed. To reduce outward swellings and ease pain, a paste can be made with the flowers and applied to bruises and sprains.

Cleavers

This herb is considered a purifier of the blood. The old ones create a spring drink for purification. It has many uses. Make an ointment and use for scalds or ulcerated skin or make a wash for sunburns if applied with a soft cloth. Express the juice to take internally for obstructions of the bladder or for cancer. It is not recommended for someone suffering from diabetes. It is an abundant plant that grows wild. The seeds are encased in little burrs that stick to anything, which helps to spread them.

Coltsfoot

This plant has antibacterial properties useful for coughs and asthma. The plant appears early in the spring before the dandelions. The flowers are on the stems with no apparent leaves. Be careful with the dosage, it can be toxic and cause liver problems.

Comfrey

A common name is knit bone. A common use of this plant is as a poultice for serious injuries. It has analgesic properties and soothes wounds and helps to heal cuts and bruises. It can also be taken as a tea and is soothing for diarrhea, bleeding gums, ulcers, and stomach complaints. The leaves are large and soft, resembling in size and shape a non-glossy dock leaf. The commonly lilac flowers bloom through the summer. The plant grows in partial shade, usually under a hedge or at the edge of a wood.

Dandelion   This plant is used as a liver tonic. The leaves are ideal for flushing stones out from the kidneys and urinary tract. They help stabilize hypoglycemia, and have a diuretic action and promote digestion. This plant can be helpful in treating a lack of appetite and indigestion. It is also used to promote weight loss. The root contains bitters and is good for cleansing the liver, spleen and gallbladder. It is useful in the treatment of jaundice, hepatitis, and the early stages of cirrhosis. The sap is used externally as a remedy for warts. The sap is best collected after the frost has gone.

Elderberry   This tree is very common in Ireland. It grows in hedges and alongside the roads. During the summer the beautiful cream flowers have a strong scent. These are followed by clusters of blackberries in the autumn. Useful as an antioxidant, the berries will help support the immune system. All parts of the tree are usable. The most important use is for relieving congestion. It is also used to treat flu, coughs, bacterial and viral infections, tonsillitis, hay fever and is used to improve vision. It also can be used to control diarrhea.

Foxglove

This plant is used to treat heart disease. It is highly poisonous and is used in minute quantities. It has purple and white flowers. When plants are young they look like a comfrey plant but smaller.

Fennel

This plant is a good remedy for the digestive system particularly to treat flatulence, abdominal cramps, congestion, and colic. It is especially suitable for children. It helps to increase milk in nursing mothers while at the same time treating the colic in the baby. A solution made from the seeds can be good for eye infections.

Ferns (Filices)

This plant eases colic. It is also used in the treatment of bruises and bones that are broken or out of joint. Either make a concoction to drink, or an ointment, or boil in oil for external application.

Flax Seed

Is used as a cancer treatment, especially for breast and prostate cancer. It is also helpful with blood sugar regulation for diabetes and reduces the risk of heart attack.

Fumitory

Taken internally it is a diuretic that is used to treat the gall bladder. External uses included a tonic for milk crust on the scalp of children.

Ground Ivy	The leaves are brewed into a tea for coughs, tuberculosis and to prepare a digestive tonic. Anciently it was used to brew beer before hops were imported. It is an inflammatory that can be used to relieve fever and pains including earache and toothache. Mix with yarrow or chamomile as a poultice on abscesses, boils, ulcers and rashes. Extract the juice and sniff up the nose to clear congestion and ease headaches. It can cure jaundice and eczema. It is found at the edge of the woods or under hedges.
Guelde Rose	This shrub grows between five to ten feet high, has large maple-like leaves with snowy white flowers in the summer and bright red berries in August. The berries have been used for ink. The shrub is an antispasmodic, used to treat asthma and prevent miscarriage. It is an uterine relaxant. The dried bark is used for cramps.
Hawthorn	This plant nourishes the blood. It is used in treating poor circulation, hardening of the arteries and congestive heart failure. It also successfully reduces high blood pressure, angina and palpitations. The dried berries are also used as a digestive aid. It was considered unlucky to bring the bush into the house. The beautiful clusters of white flowers are seen in May. The branches are thorny with small glossy dark

green leaves. When the flowers die, the berries or haws gradually appear.

Horsetail	Is one of the oldest plants in existence. It is a wound healer and used for staunching bleeding both externally and internally. It has been used to treat stomach ulcers, bleeding from the womb, nose and bladder as well as discharges from the lungs, prostate, and urinary systems. It is also used as a diuretic. It can be used to treat sores and chilblains, which are skin ulcers usually on the feet and hands brought on by exposure to cold and humidity.
Irish Moss (Seaweed)	This particular seaweed is used to treat sore throats, chapped skin, goiters, and other thyroid diseases. It contains iodine. It is also used as a mild laxative. It can be used externally as a hot seaweed bath for aches and pains associated with rheumatism and arthritis. It can also be used to treat poor skin conditions.
Meadowsweet	This plant has clusters of cream or pale yellow flowers. It is mainly for pain relief but is also used to treat urinary infections. It kills bacteria. It is also a diarrhea treatment and a remedy for acid stomach. It is safe to use and has no harmful side effects. Even cats will drink it.
Mistletoe	This plant is used in the treatment of respiratory diseases and the treatment of cancer.

Motherwort	This plant has a sedative effect. It has been used for the prevention of pregnancy and to bring on menses. It is used during labour to ease anxiety and labour pains. It is also used as a uterine tonic after delivery to help prevent infection. It is not to be used during pregnancy as it may cause bleeding. It has also been used to treat skin cancer.
Nettles	This plant is an anti-inflammatory and will ease the pain of gout and the pains of joints and sinews. It also helps stop bleeding. It is also helpful in drawing out splinters. Making an infusion to be taken internally, it is used to treat asthma, coughs, and pneumonia. Cooking the leaves neutralizes the sting. Traditionally it was used in May as a blood purifier. Three meals a day of boiled nettles were taken for three days. If this was not done, it was believed that older ones were more liable to suffer strokes and heart attacks.
Parsley	This herb is an ideal source of iron and Vitamin C. It is also used as a dressing on wounds and for conjunctivitis. The juice from the crushed leaves is useful for getting rid of head lice. It is a diuretic and muscle relaxant. It can be used to treat migraines, asthma, stomach cramps, bladder weakness, painful periods, kidney diseases or ulcers. Since it stimulates muscles, using parsley can bring on delayed menstruation. It is good to take

after childbirth, but should be used sparingly during pregnancy.

Plantain

This plant is also called Ribwort. It is considered a liver protector. It is used as a diuretic, and aids in treating high cholesterol and is an astringent. The leaves will stay the bleeding of minor wounds. As a soothing salve, it has good drawing properties in treating sores and skin ulcers when used under a dressing. Traditionally the leaves were placed in the bottom of shoes to help with blisters and bruises.

Roseroot

This small shrub with its delicate yellow flower grows in the mountains. The flowers can be harvested from May to August, and the seeds from July to August. For over 3,000 years it has been used to treat fatigue and stress induced symptoms. It regulates hormones. It is reported to have an enhancing effect upon physical endurance and sexual potency. It is used raw or cooked.

Silver Birch

The leaves can be harvested in spring and dried for later use. They are known as an anti-virus and an anti-tumor remedy. The inner bark can be distilled and used for fevers. Oil from the inner bark is an astringent used for skin afflictions. An infusion of the leaves is a dissolvent of kidney stones and used for the treatment of gout and rheumatism.

St. John's Wort	This plant has five petaled bright yellow flowers found growing up through the grass along the roadside. It is used in the treatment of depression, obsessive compulsive disorder, shingles, bed-wetting, epilepsy, and menopausal symptoms. It strengthens the nervous system and gives a sense of well being.
Thyme	This herb is an anti-spasmodic of the smooth muscles. It is also an antiseptic used to medicate bandages. The oil is good for fungal and parasitic infections. To relieve the pain of an abscess, a paste of hot moistened leaves can be applied locally. Infuse it in water for coughs and bronchitis. Gargle three times a day to improve throat infections. It was used as a treatment for whooping cough. In the stomach it helps the digestive system and is useful for flatulence. It can help in the treatment of a diseased liver. It is useful in the treatment of childrens' asthma, loss of appetite, nightmares and restless sleep.
Valerian Root	This plant is a wild flower native to Ireland. It is a tall plant with small pale pink flowers. It is found growing by streams and damp places. It is an anti-spasmodic commonly used for sedation and sleep disorders. It also relieves menstrual pains, headaches, migraines, epileptic tendencies and abdominal pain. It has been used to treat asthma, colitis and dyspepsia. It can be washed, dried at low temperatures, chopped into small pieces

and stored in an airtight jar. When required for use, the pieces can be ground into a powder. They should be macerated in cold water overnight and then made into an infusion.

Willow Bark	The bark is an anti-inflammatory. It is not for the treatment of children. Common uses are for the treatment of low-back pain, headache, bursitis and tendonitis. Chewing on the bark will also reduce fever and inflammation.
Yarrow	This plant has feathery leaves with white flowers. The illness beneficial list is almost endless: staunching wounds and nosebleeds, relief of gout, rheumatism, toothache, intestinal problems, kidney, liver, gall bladder, heart and circulation, gynecological problems, regulation of menstruation, recovery from fever and colds, early treatment of diabetes and malaria. It can be used for relaxing in a bath and a cleansing lotion for greasy skin.
Yellow Dock	This root has an high iron content. It is a mild laxative that works within a few hours. It will benefit the digestive tract. Do not use while pregnant or nursing.

Family Group Record for Paddy and Mary Doherty

Husband	Patrick "Big Paddy Newman" Doherty		
Born	1838	Ballyloskey, Carndonagh, County Donegal, Ireland	
Christened			
Died	10 Nov 1919	Carndonagh, Inishowen, County Donegal, Ulster, Ireland	
Buried		Sacred Heart Church, Carndonagh, County Donegal, Ireland	
Father	Philip "Newman" Doherty		
Mother	Nancy McLaughlin		
Marriage	15 May 1869	Carndonagh, Inishowen, County Donegal, Ulster, Ireland	

Wife	Mary "Hudie" Doherty		
Born	1847	Ballyloskey, Carndonagh, County Donegal, Ireland	
Christened			
Died	27 Mar 1932	Carndonagh, Inishowen, County Donegal, Ulster, Ireland	
Buried		Sacred Heart Church, Carndonagh, County Donegal, Ireland	
Father	John "Shoemaker" Doherty		
Mother	Catherine Granny		

Children

1	F	Mary "Newman" Doherty	
Born	20 Aug 1870	Ballyloskey, Carndonagh, County Donegal, Ireland	
Christened			
Died	1873	Carndonagh, Inishowen, County Donegal, Ulster, Ireland	
Buried			
Spouse	Did Not Marry		

2	F	Catherine M. "Katie Newman" Doherty	
Born	7 Mar 1872	Ballyloskey, Carndonagh, County Donegal, Ireland	
Christened			
Died	7 Apr 1952	Heppner, Morrow County, Oregon, USA	
Buried			
Spouse	James Grant Doherty	6 Jul 1893 - Pendleton, Umatilla County, Oregon, USA	

3	M	Philip "Newman" Doherty	
Born	31 Oct 1874	Ballyloskey, Carndonagh, County Donegal, Ireland	
Christened			
Died	9 Feb 1946	Heppner, Morrow County, Oregon, USA	
Buried	14 Feb 1946	Heppner, Morrow County, Oregon, USA	
Spouse	Margaret McDaid	30 Dec 1900 - Heppner, Morrow County, Oregon, USA	

4	F	Anne "Newman" Doherty	
Born	17 May 1876	Ballyloskey, Carndonagh, County Donegal, Ireland	
Christened			
Died	20 Dec 1898	Butter Creek, Heppner, Morrow County, Oregon, USA	
Buried		Pendleton, Umatilla County, Oregon, USA	
Spouse	Edward "Glenkeen" Doherty	29 Dec 1896 - Heppner, Morrow County, Oregon, USA	

Family Group Record for Paddy and Mary Doherty

Children (cont.)

5	M	John P. "Newman" Doherty	
AKA		Dutchy Doherty	
Born		6 Feb 1878	Ballyloskey, Carndonagh, County Donegal, Ireland
Christened			
Died		1956	Heppner, Morrow County, Oregon, USA
Buried			Heppner, Morrow County, Oregon, USA
Spouse		Did Not Marry	

6	M	Paul "Newman" Doherty	
AKA		Old Paul Doherty	
Born		5 May 1880	Ballyloskey, Carndonagh, County Donegal, Ireland
Christened			
Died		10 Sep 1962	Carndonagh, Inishowen, County Donegal, Ulster, Ireland
Buried			
Spouse		Mary McCallion	3 Feb 1910 - Carndonagh, Inishowen, County Donegal, Ulster, Ireland

7	M	Bernard "Newman" Doherty	
Born		4 Jun 1882	Ballyloskey, Carndonagh, County Donegal, Ireland
Christened			
Died		Jun 1882	Carndonagh, Inishowen, County Donegal, Ulster, Ireland
Buried			
Spouse		Did Not Marry	

8	M	Eugene "Newman" Doherty	
Born		2 Jan 1884	Ballyloskey, Carndonagh, County Donegal, Ireland
Christened			
Died		16 Nov 1950	Fairbanks, North Star County, Alaska, USA
Buried			Heppner, Morrow County, Oregon, USA
Spouse		Did Not Marry	

9	F	Ellen Nora "Nora Newman" Doherty	
AKA		Nora Doherty	
Born		23 Jun 1886	Ballyloskey, Carndonagh, County Donegal, Ireland
Christened			
Died		1 Jul 1916	Heppner, Morrow County, Oregon, USA
Buried			
Spouse		Francis McCabe	2 Jun 1907 - Heppner, Morrow County, Oregon, USA

Family Group Record for Paddy and Mary Doherty

Children (cont.)		
10 **F**	**Sarah "Sadie Newman" Doherty**	
AKA	Sadie Doherty	
Born	11 Jan 1888	Ballyloskey, Carndonagh, County Donegal, Ireland
Christened		
Died	1 Jun 1937	Carndonagh, Inishowen, County Donegal, Ulster, Ireland
Buried		
Spouse	Patrick "Paddy Curley" Kearney	
Marr. Date	24 Jun 1923 - Carndonagh, Inishowen, County Donegal, Ulster, Ireland	
11 **F**	**Rose "Rosie Newman" Doherty**	
AKA	Rosie Doherty	
Born	27 Aug 1890	Ballyloskey, Carndonagh, County Donegal, Ireland
Christened		
Died	2 Apr 1965	Walla Walla, Walla Walla County, Washington, USA
Buried	5 Apr 1965	Masonic Cemetery, Heppner, Morrow County, Oregon, USA
Spouse	William Thomas "Willie Tom Mary Willie" Doherty	
Marr. Date	26 Feb 1924 - Heppner, Morrow County, Oregon, USA	
12 **F**	**Margaret "Maggie Newman" Doherty**	
Born	11 May 1892	Ballyloskey, Carndonagh, County Donegal, Ireland
Christened		
Died	2 Jan 1982	Renton, King County, Washington, USA
Buried		Mt. Olivet Cemetery, Renton, King County, Washington, USA
Spouse	Michael Joseph Creegan	23 Sep 1917 - Portland, Multnomah County, Oregon, USA

225

Local map of Carndonagh and Ballyloskey

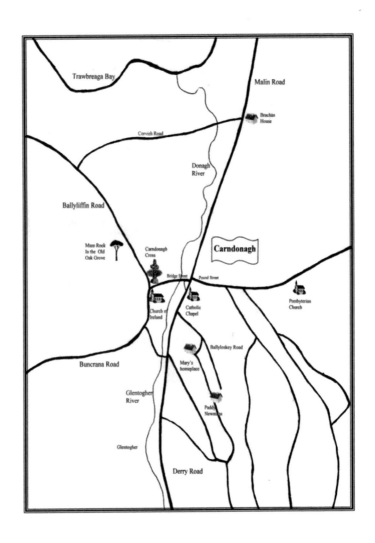

Trawbreaga Bay

Malin Road

Brachín House

Corvish Road

Donagh River

Ballyliffin Road

Mass Rock In the Old Oak Grove

Carndonagh Cross

Carndonagh

Bridge Street

Pound Street

Presbyterian Church

Church of Ireland

Catholic Chapel

Ballyloskey Road

Mary's homeplace

Buncrana Road

Glentogher River

Paddy Newins

Glentogher

Derry Road

map of inishowen, county donegal and derry city, county derry, ireland

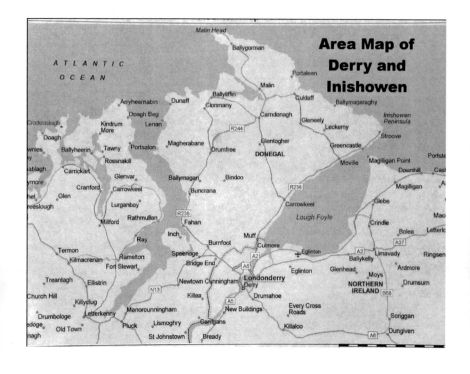